JUST AVERAGE?

A LADY BOOMER'S ODYSSEY

Hi, Beth,
I hope you enjoy
my semi-fictional memoir –
"JA" – after all "Fun is
a Personal Responsibility,"
yeah? + I think you'll
recognize my "reorgination"
story 🙂 my friend!

Allison Seaborn
July 2018

JUST AVERAGE?

A LADY BOOMER'S ODYSSEY

Allison Seaborn

The New Atlantian Library

The New Atlantian Library
is an imprint of
ABSOLUTELY AMAZING eBOOKS

Published by Whiz Bang LLC, 926 Truman Avenue, Key West, Florida 33040, USA.

For information contact:
Publisher@AbsolutelyAmazingEbooks.com

ISBN-13: 978-1945772030 (The New Atlantian Library)
ISBN-10: 1945772034

DEDICATED TO:

My Dad, Gerald "Blaine" Seaborn ("To the Captain!)

And

My Mom, "Connie" Swanson Seaborn (The Tiger of
Ingalton School)
And

Buddy – A Friend Forever!

JUST AVERAGE?

A LADY BOOMER'S ODYSSEY

Introduction

"*L*ady Boomers" is a term I created for female baby boomers who, as you know, were born between 1946 and 1964. Whether we are corporate managers, administrative assistants earning middle-class wages, stay-at-home grandmas or international travelers, we are readers with discretionary incomes. Those of us in our 50s and 60s need – and deserve – something to lighten our lives after a long, demanding day, whether reading online or in hand.

Just Average? is semiautobiographical – or perhaps even more specifically – a semi-fictional memoir with a lot of humor. Topics include self-esteem, dating, finances, parenting adult children, conflict, friendship and more, which are intertwined with feelings of being very ordinary, "just average," and past my prime. After all, we were raised with modesty as a virtue. Aren't our children far more talented than we could ever be? Why would a hot guy want me now? And, how can I plan retirement – I don't even know what I want to be when I grow up!

Even though the readers' experiences won't be exactly the same as mine, their odysseys – "a long wandering or series of travel" – will resonate with the emotions and questions we have in common. Whether a reader embraces these steps is, of course, at her discretion.

Through a compilation of characters – some from the past and others more recent, and with exaggerated situations – some quirky – some poignant – some downright risqué – I change my mind about who I am. I come to believe that fun is a personal responsibility. It's up to me to choose to feel good about myself. I also realize that my professional skills are not just "common sense." I have unique talents and experiences, and I'm damn good at what I do. By consciously applying mental adjustments, such as changing "bad'itudes" – bad attitudes – into "glad'itudes" – positive attitudes, life can be easier and richer.

- Allison Seaborn

Chapter 1

IT'S GOTTA GO

KICK STARTING THE SECOND HALF

*H*i. You caught me madly typing. I'm not sure whether I should take off my bra to be more comfortable or plunge right in and tell you my story. How did I get to this time of life? How can I be beyond middle age and still don't know what I want to be when I grow up?

Now that I'm the parent of adult children, I find myself asking, "How did my life segue from the personal exploration of my own youthful hopes and dreams to being far more invested in theirs? When did I come to think my achievement potential was just average, but they could reach for the stars?"

It all came to a head after I watched a super star's TV bio. Honestly, that could have been my kid up there. My daughter is, after all, Academy Award material. She was raised in Los Angeles but had neglected an acting career. Instead, she's studying to be a doctor or scientist – which aren't bad ideas – and she will have the opportunity to go her own way.

But can a Nobel Prize compete with an Academy Award in stature?

Why was I more focused on her professional success than my own?

As a wannabe stage mother, I had to learn about letting go the hard way. Ever since she was a toddler, I knew my curly-haired darling was the next Shirley Temple in tennis shoes. When she got a call to try out for a commercial or movie role, I would prepare her as best I could.

"Sparkle, baby, sparkle!" I used to say.

Her natural inclination for acting even showed itself the day she graduated from high school. She walked jauntily across the grassy field to accept her diploma, holding her gown above her knees and kicking her bare feet joyously in the air.

Suddenly, my daughter was grown up, eighteen years old and free to go to limitless auditions at any time of the day. Her agent asked her to be in "the book" of promising young talent all the casting directors kept handy.

But she followed her passion and left for college instead – dumped Hollywood for Minnesota, her birthplace.

My son, on the other hand, hated school, "...except for the girls." He was born in Key West, Florida. He's a "Conch," as people born there are called. It's a tradition from the old days when the arrival of a baby was announced by placing a conch shell in the yard.

After his dad and I split, I took the kid to Minnesota where I was raised. He grew up on a freshwater fishing paradise north of Minneapolis. He fished year-round and bragged about his most memorable ice fishing experience whenever anyone would listen.

He was in his portable ice fishing house when a burst of strong wind tumbled it across the lake. "I grabbed the stringer of fish, and after we got done rolling around, I still had it," he finishes with a proud grin. He's definitely a great storyteller!

As a teen, he started spending part of his summers in Key West and learned commercial fishing from his Dad.

Years later, he asked me if I wanted to hear a funny story about school. As the naïve mother of an adult child, I ignorantly nodded. My smile faded as I learned he had spent several days of his senior year playing hooky with his fishing buddies. They'd hop on the school bus in the morning, only to get off on the other side of the lake a few minutes later. At the end of a fun-filled day, they'd get back on the bus and ride home. Then, they'd forge each other's parental excuse notes and get away with it.

His grades suffered, of course. But, to him a "C" average was not just average. He didn't want to go to college or work in a windowless corporate cube. His stated goal was: "No desk, no tie, no meetings." His time was better invested in skipping school and cutting bait.

Ironically, the kid who got into the most trouble in high school was the most studious, an open-minded exchange student from India. His host family was proud of him – his test scores as a senior were off the charts.

But the independent longhair committed the sin of peacefully sitting on the floor in a school hallway, playing his sitar and leading classmates in a protest over the music program. He was frustrated that the school offered no opportunity to introduce his idol – Ravi Shankar – into their lives. The principal heard about it and came down the hallway, eyes bulging and spit flying. He yelled at the kid and ordered him to "Knock it off!" or he'd be expelled.

When "that kid" graduated as valedictorian of his class, he deliberately tripped on the stage. Just to take some of the pomp out of the ceremony. Just to piss off the principal.

The students were all laughing and cheering, "Ravi! Ravi! Ravi!" Being a '60s kid myself, I was proud to join in.

We all think our kids are superstars. We brag about them as we confidently urge them forward.

Yet my friends and I, though somewhat proud of our own successes, feel overall pretty ordinary. We lady baby boomers – "lady boomers" for short – are now in our 50s and 60s. We had been raised in an era where acting modest was a virtue. But had we internalized that attitude? Did we genuinely admire each other's personal and professional accomplishments while mentally downplaying our own?

Just as we are too hard on ourselves when it comes to our own body image, we often devalue our own skills. Are ours "good" while others' are "better" and "best"? Do we discourage ourselves by wallowing in what we *should* have done – or *can't* do?

I was once congratulating an old flame of mine on his expertise at poker, admiring his nerve to stay in the game. Me, I get a stomachache when I lost five dollars. I was grousing about how conservative I was, yet how brave he was.

He looked at me in surprise and commented, "I know how to play poker and count cards. It's not that much of a risk for me. I win most of the time. But I could never do what you did – trek around Europe for six weeks exploring your ancestry."

I did have a self-confident friend, a legal secretary who thought she was better than one of the world's sexiest movie stars. Remember that famous "One Million Years B.C." poster with Raquel Welch in the doeskin bikini? Along with every other woman over the age of 12, I was lamenting about ordinary me compared to gorgeous her. My practical friend patiently responded, "She gets paid to exercise. I bet I can type better." Awesome!

That was an eye-opener! Maybe I didn't have to come in last when comparing myself to someone else.

Like so many lady boomers, I'll bet you shrug off your unique skills, assuming that everyone can do what you do. Trust me, they can't. I have a rocket scientist friend – literally, he's a rocket scientist – who can't figure out how to put up a Christmas tree!

If *that's* true, *then* it's O.K. – positive – for me to say to myself and you that *I* am great at what *I* do – teaching at community colleges and working at nonprofits.

It's still O.K. if I can't sing like some of you, or if I never took physics. One time, I volunteered to help paint a couple of rooms in a friend's house, thinking it would be easy. But I was real sore the next day from jumping on and off a ladder to stretch up, crouch down. How does someone do that hour after hour, day after day? Or, run a farm? Or, sketch a portrait?

I did drive a big truck cross-country once. Everything I owned was in the 24-foot box of that truck, with my car being pulled behind it. By the time I got a few hundred miles up the road, I realized the so-called "friends" who were supposed to help me move had flaked out. I didn't even know how to back up the rig, so I had to keep moving forward. It was hard, but I made it. I even earned a new handle: "Mother Trucker." Strange as that tale is, I've got a new respect for truckers. As with most things we only see from a distance, it ain't as easy as it looks!

We don't see our own talents clearly. We think of them as easily acquired or plain old common sense. *Wrong!*

We need an attitude adjustment!

Common sense ain't so common, so let's get rid of that "Aw, shucks" mentality. Let's quit responding to compliments by smiling modestly, lowering our eyes slightly and murmuring, "Gee, thanks, but it really wasn't such a big deal..." Let's stop putting ourselves down. Let's give ourselves all the kudos we deserve – we earned 'em – we'll take 'em.

I know! We'll adopt a new motto:

"Just say, 'Thank you'."

That simple acknowledgment will show off our newfound confidence. And the more self-assured we feel, the easier it will be to praise others. They will respond by saying, "Thank you," and we'll follow-up with a sincere,

"You're welcome!" Just think of the ripple effect!

I don't know the dreams and accomplishments that are part of you, but I do believe that our goals are measurable stepping-stones in life's journey. Whether small or huge, simple or intimidating, the value we personally place on each success determines our reward. We are our *own* goaltenders.

Sometimes it takes a long time to reach an important goal. As a girl growing up in Minnesota in the '60s, I was raised to believe a college degree was the path to a successful career. But it would take me 15 years to get one.

I'd graduated from high school with honors when I was 17. That fall, I attended college right on schedule, with my parents paying for everything. I had it made.

Only, there was a sneaky changetaking place. No longer "the good girl," my wild side took over when I moved off campus my sophomore year. Parties with pizza and beer made going to morning classes a struggle. Then, what the heck, I'd blow off the entire day. Finally, I just quit going altogether.

During that time I got to know a classmate who was also ready for recess. She was a lot of fun, and she even had her own car! We started hanging out together. Maybe it was bad karma, but we ended up getting into a skirmish with the police. It was all innocent, I swear.

It happened one night when were driving home for the weekend and decided to visit a miniature golf course where my younger brother – "Li'l Bro" – worked. We decided to play and were having a great time until we hit the "Land of Lakes" hole. My friend's ball plopped into the water hazard. Being a good sport, she grinned ear to ear and jumped right into the water after the ball. She slipped on the bottom slime and got soaked. All the guys really appreciated the sight. She was exceptionally well endowed and may have been the inspiration for wet t-shirt contests.

Changing into a long-sleeved button down shirt she'd just bought, she casually hung the uncomfortable wet bra on the car's side view mirror to dry in the wind.

We drove through the local root beer stand on the east side of the cruise loop. Nothing was happening, so we continued cruising to the other end of town for burgers. We were sitting in a red, fake leather booth, laughing over our dumb day. From the way the waitress nervously dropped our food on the table and backed away, we figured we were being loud and obnoxious. The stuffy hostess glared as we left. Certainly, my friend's shirt drew attention to us.

Did I mention that it was an institutional blue one with large block letters: "PROPERTY OF STATE PRISON #0069"? Or that it was a tad tight across her chest?

We pulled on to the highway back into town, and BAM! Four squad cars forced us over. One in front and one in back, with two more blocking the lane next to us. With sirens blaring and a million revolving lights flashing into the car, they had us pinned. Busted! Big time!

"Get your bra off the mirror!" I shouted to my friend. She reached out and snagged it, tossing the wet lump on the seat between us. Having no idea what the hell was happening, we didn't gawk – we just stared in amazement.

The police approached, guns drawn, and ordered us to "Put your hands up!" Just like in the movies! Of course, neither of us had ever experienced anything like this before. Our hands shot into the air, but when my braless friend put her hands up the button on the front of her shirt popped off. She automatically put her hands down to cover up. The angry cop got louder when he shouted, "Get those hands back up!" She did, but more than her cleavage was now exposed. Being a nice middle-class girl – more or less – her modesty overcame the danger and she again put her hands over her bosom.

7

By the third time she was ordered to reach for the sky, the cops had gone through our car, feeling around with their flashlights in hand. Satisfied that we had no weapons, they ordered us to follow them to the station. The embarrassing caravan proceeded right down Main Street.

Inside the station, they finally revealed our suspected transgression. We resembled escapees from the state reformatory. The hostess at the restaurant had called the law: the #0069 shirt was the big tip-off.

I looked up at one of the officers and said, "I have that same shirt in the trunk of the car. We bought them today at a discount store. Mine's still in the bag."

Looking doubtful, the boss man assigned one of his boys to check it out. Since my friend was hunched, arms crossed, sulking in a chair, it was up to me to unlock the trunk for the detective. Peeking in, he saw the plastic bag. He gingerly took out my shirt. Holding it officially up to his nose, he sniffed.

"Smells new."

Closest thing to an analytical genius I'd ever seen.

As we walked back inside, he returned my driver's license by stuffing it slowly and snugly into my front shirt pocket as he leered at my chest. "Here you go, missy," the slime ball winked, coming on with the attitude of a sly cad – a definite "cad'itude."

I swatted his hand away and snapped, "You say something before you start pickin' around!"

Things calmed down a little, and they let us go.

In retrospect, it's probably a good thing we got hauled in. Otherwise, we'd have been across the state line. My friend and I had spontaneously decided that very night to head down to Key West, Florida, in search of a carefree, fun lifestyle.

We took the trek south the following summer.

I got a job at a pool hall. It didn't take long for me to fall in love with an irresistible guy I met there. He was an adventurer and a fisherman. His entire left calf was one massive scar where a shark tried to bite off his leg! As if that weren't impressive enough, he was also a romantic poet.

His idol was Ernest Hemingway, whose old island home was now a museum. But rumor had it that when Hemingway needed solitude, he escaped by boat to an unknown hideaway in the Gulf of Mexico on the west side of the island. Somehow, my poet knew where it was, and he took me a few miles off shore to a sand bar. There in the shallow waters was an awe-inspiring old wooden shack on stilts. It was falling apart. I now fully believed him when he said the great author had come to him in a dream to tell him about this secret place.

I was smitten. We got married.

Our island paradise was warm, mellow and affordable in the '60s. It was a different world, and we flowed freely. In our bare feet, we tripped from the Gulf end of the island to the eastern Atlantic side without touching the sidewalk. Imagine taking all day for an adventure like that!

We used to hang out on Mallory Dock, a concrete and wood structure on the Gulf side. It was a quiet spot in those days. Three or four people during any given evening were considered a crowd. Occasionally, there was a kid who would show up and dive off the dock for the coins we threw. One night, my man felt the inspiration to liven things up and do a little fishing. I'd been raised around Minnesota's freshwater lakes, but saltwater fishing was new to me. I was excited and eager to get going.

"The Cutlass," our crazy Navy friend stationed in the Keys, joined us in the adventure. He got his nickname from the sword earring he wore when he ditched his uniform for playtime.

Right after sunset, my poet put a chunk of bonito on a heavy handline with a chain hook rig. He swung it in circles over his head several times and heaved it out to sea. After a couple of quiet hours, there was a tremendous tug. He thought it was a giant jewfish, which were frequently caught there. Little by little, we pulled the monster in closer. But there was a major setback when it swam around a wooden piling about 40 yards out from the dock.

Our fearless friend offered to swim across the deep water in the dark to untangle the line. Jumping in, The Cutlass swam the distance, guided by moonlight.

About half way out, he shouted, "I can feel the fish with my feet. Man, I'm damn near riding it!" He worked the line loose from the pilings and swam back to the dock, exhilarated. We pulled in the fish. One look, and we about shit where we stood.

The Cutlass had been swimming on top of a 13-foot hammerhead shark!

As word got out in the morning hours, locals and tourists gathered, staring at the shark in amazement. The rows of razor-sharp teeth could slice you in half. A newspaper reporter arrived to take a picture and write the story. He informed us that the Smithsonian was searching for a big hammerhead and was willing to pay.

By then it was too late. We had already cut out the jaws – which nearly fit over our shoulders.

All in all, it was an incredibly exciting night. When my poet and I got home, we sat on our apartment's balcony watching the town wake up. Although we were tired, we were experiencing an amazing adrenaline high. I looked up at him to see him looking down at me. Grabbing each other, we tumbled off our chairs. Nine months later our son was born.

I often reflect fondly on that passionate morning, and on that small window of time in young adulthood when we felt rebellious and free. Back when we were flower children during the Summer of Love.

Didn't you have your flash of freedom in your 20's? I thought every generation did. I came to learn, however, that my Dad's didn't. He and his buddies had turned 20 during the worst year of the Great Depression. The same year that FDR told them, "The only thing we have to fear, is fear itself." Rather than nonchalantly tripping around, they worked on the family farm and dreamt of someday replacing the frayed collars on their shirts.

His generation had grit, though. When money was short and the tractor needed fixing, they put it right with bailing wire and inspiration.

"How's it going?" a neighboring farmer would ask.

"It's gotta go," was the resolute reply.

Being in the fresh air and working the land was in my father's blood. The feel of the soil beneath his fingernails and the sweat staining his brow at the end of a hard day's toil made more sense to him than wearing a suit and tie.

But changes were happening, and he began to explore and develop interest in another field of work. He made a decision and, when he was able to go, Dad went to college in the city and earned a degree in chemical engineering. He became a successful oil company salesman and, ironically, finished his career as a pollution control manager.

Yet all through those years, Dad took a solitary drive into the country every Saturday to replenish his soul. It was years after he died before I understood that pilgrimage.

My Dad couldn't be trapped inside – he still needed time out in the sun and sky.

My son stubbornly stuck to his path – "No desk, no tie, no meetings."

The salt was in the boy's blood, and after high school

he moved back to the island of Key West where it all began. The only thing he doesn't like about being a sportfishing captain is when a hurricane threat drives away the tourists, and he finds himself stranded on land for more than a day.

His job is to take his clients out fishing and catching, and enjoys them feeling like the "best hook" of the day. One especially memorable charter was a visiting president from a small foreign country. He had booked a half-day afternoon trip, and my son had been advised the feds would begin a security inspection of his boat about an hour ahead of time. He and his deck assistant – the "first mate" – were looking forward to an excellent trip with the esteemed dignitary.

Sounds simple, but the adventure began a little earlier than expected.

Anticipation turned to dread as he was bringing in the six passengers from the morning fishing charter. Despite the "No Drugs" sign prominently displayed on the outside of the cabin, these amateurs decided to relax and light up a joint. With a drug- and bomb-sniffing security dog waiting on the dock, the timing couldn't have been worse.

Being a sportfishing captain on the ocean only looks like it's fun all the time. But, it's a Coast Guard licensed profession, and any trace of that illegal marijuana on board meant my son could lose the boat and his captain's license. His livelihood could go down the drain for a bunch of stoners. The fools were snotty to him when he explained the situation. They had to stop. They refused.

"You gotta be tough when you're dumb," grumbled the disgusted mate.

All it took was one quick radio call to the authorities, and the stoned tourists were offloaded to a Coast Guard vessel.

As soon as the charter boat got back to the dock, the

planned security check began. My son explained the tourists and their marijuana. The dog sniffed out the weed residue topside, and the agent contacted the Coast Guard to confirm.

At the same time, two divers swam underneath the boat to ensure security. Then, the president came aboard, accompanied by a heavily armed agent. As they headed out to sea, boats appeared both port and starboard. Each carried feds with guns and a diver fully poised for action with one leg over the side. Just to be safe, a helicopter flew overhead.

The president was relaxed, though, accustomed to the presence of security personnel. He caught some damn fine fish and booked another trip.

That's just one example of the many experiences my "I don't want to go to college" son has enjoyed. The boat he's currently running is one of the top for mounting game fish. Famous athletes look to *him* for expert advice. Wow! When you let 'em fly, they soar!

My little boy had gone after his trophies his own way.

Then he lured me back to Florida with a persuasive, "Come on, Mom, and help raise your grandson."

Emotionally, I wanted to, but it took about a year to convince my logical side.

At that time, I was working in California, where I was on the righteous path to a lifetime of financial security. If you've ever moved cross country without a new job in hand, you know you're faced with starting over. Your finances take a vertical dive, and you struggle as you spend your hard-earned savings until you can nail a "real" job. The more career breaks you take, the less you build for retirement. More = less.

I loved the work I was currently doing at a wonderful nonprofit organization, but my awesome boss had retired. Her supervisory style was an inspiration. She began the hiring process by hand picking individuals with vitality, skill and dig-in dedication. Then, she'd charge us with creating something from scratch. As intimidating as that responsibility could be, she trusted us to get the job done. I felt tremendously creative working under her. I was disappointed when she retired.

Then I freaked when I learned the leadership style of my new boss.

She approached her "work" as a micromanager. She ranked toward the bottom. It went something like this: when I was assigned to create a grant proposal for funding to get a new program off the ground, I tackled that proverbial "blank page" with energy and self-discipline. Revisions, though necessary, were a piece of cake by comparison.

But I was derailed at every corner by this hysterical 30-something boss who wouldn't listen to a word I had to say. The kind who marched about clutching her red ink pen like a life preserver, making micro – "small, petty..." – changes. This is according to the ultimate authority in language usage – "Gram's '49" –my grandmother's 1949 *Webster's New Collegiate Dictionary*, formally marked, "Property of the Stenographic Department."

She was the kind of boss who was so intimidated by making decisions about the bigger picture she kept busy producing multiple versions with trivial changes. So her nose was in everything.

Imagine a boss who "happens" to pass by your office and peeks her head in the door, pretending to be professionally friendly. In actuality, she's scrutinizing your desktop and what's on your computer screen.

If she's satisfied you're not checking personal phone messages or playing computer card games, she'll give you a transparently fake greeting, as if you're her best pal: "Hey, lady!" The weird part is, instead of three syllables of similar time, it sounds like she practiced at home on her piano: "Hey" is held for two counts on middle C, and slides down to G. "Lady" then bounces from middle C up to D.

On the other hand, if you don't appear busy enough, she gives you a brisk, staccato, "Hi-I- see-you're-busy-so-I-won't-bother-you." It's ripe with oddly combined C sharps, B flats, Cs and Ds. She may even scan the thank-you letter you're creating on the computer, nitpicking worse than usual.

Meanwhile, the proposal you created, whether to help needy families, manufacture a new gardening tool, design a unique dress or whatever, never gets Out The Door.

None of this made sense to my micromanager – and she wasn't going to change for me. She was in charge and, as we know, the boss always wins.

Well, then – what good is it? OTD, that's the key.

The problem was that I wasn't finding ads or references for jobs I was truly interested in. I wanted to move forward in this awesome career. Instead, I found myself applying for jobs I didn't truly want. My lack of enthusiasm probably showed itself during interviews. I kept getting rejection letters for jobs I never would have considered under any other circumstance.

You understand what I mean. You've been in interviews where you knew you didn't want the job and were relieved to walk out, haven't you? I "know an idea" as my son used to say as a little kid. Lets us job seekers be the ones to send the rejection letters or brief emails. Here goes.

"TO: Mr. Andrew Rain Showers,next line here?ARS Company:

Thank you very much for our recent interview for the position of – (whatever silly job you don't want) – Though your company was impressive, I must decline.

It's an employees' market at this time, and I have chosen a marvelous job with a corporation whose pay scale, flexibility, benefits and stock options more closely match my needs. Good luck in your search for a dedicated worker who is willing to think inside the company box at the expense of her creativity. I know you will find the perfect fit for your ARS,

Sincerely ..."

One of my *real* choices in that environment was to change my outlook and keep working for the micro boss. But, I felt so disrespected and discouraged I knew that wouldn't work. The other option was to stay on the job and send out resumes until I got different employment. I chose the latter but that wasn't working out so well.

I'd just once like a human resources professional to ask me to give an employment reference for a previous boss. Wouldn't telling the truth be fun? But, then who wants the "little guy's" perspective? It's like those how-to-get-a-job "experts" who make millions by writing books on how to interview effectively.

Those trendsetters all say flat-out that it's crude, selfish, callous and uncaring to ask in advance for the job's salary range. The nasty implication is that part of your motivation to work for them is a paycheck.

Have you ever gone to an interview to learn later that you are miles apart on salary expectations? They wasted your time, their time, everyone's' time. What is smart about that?

Let's retaliate!

Let's tell the companies this: If you won't inform me of the pay scale for the job until after the interview, I won't let you see my resume until then either. If you are crass enough to ask about my skills, I will know you're crude, selfish, callous and uncaring, and that all you're interested in is taking advantage of my work experience. You don't give a damn about my work fulfilling me as a person. Shame on you!

Actually, job rejection is not my primary concern at this time of life. What I long for, deep in my overworked soul, is a position that can fulfill my future retirement needs.

A good friend told me there are guys at his plant who've done their time and know they're set. They continue to work only because they feel like it, as long as no one gives them any shit. They're members of the KMA – Kiss My Ass club. Oh, how I want to infiltrate that elite membership! Once there, you can patronize your boss and even turn down a promotion if you don't want the responsibility.

I'm envious and try to be a good sport over their success, but sometimes it's hard. They all know where they're going – and how to get there. Me, I'm a confused worker bee who asks herself, "How did I come to be worried about retirement? I still don't know what I want to be when I grow up." There's that bridge we lady boomers come to when we're still mulling over career options and, all of a sudden, it hits us like a thunderclap.

Our topless dancing days are over. And, furthermore, how could some of those fresh, hot actors and rock stars who were part of our young souls now be 60 or 70 or even gone?

Suddenly, an inspiration captured me! Why was I sitting around pouting, when I could be moving on to a new adventure in the tropics of south Florida?

I thought about my grandson. Though we always visited each other a couple of times a year, he was already eight years old, and I'd missed a lot of his growing up. You know how it is with little kids. They cling to you and howl when they can't go with you everywhere, even to the grocery store. Then, starting at about 11 or 12, their friends come first and mom, dad and grandma are left begging for attention.

I sold my house and packed up.

After all, I was only 50-something, and on the threshold of "middle" age as we euphemistically call it. I could transplant myself and set down new roots. I'd done it before. I was like my favorite flower – the peony. It might take me a couple of seasons to re-emerge as a full bloomer, but I was hardy and stubborn and would once again flourish. It's my habit to "drop out" every 10-15 years, anyway. I could do it again.

Maybe I was on a long-distance contact high from those pot-smoking fishermen. Once I got beyond the flower fantasy, I awoke to reality. Key West was still a fun place to visit, but in the 30-some years since I'd lived there, it had lost some of its laid-back "island attitude," especially among the city leaders. They focused became more on promoting businesses, expensive condos, crowds of tourists and t-shirt shops. It was a tough place for me to make the kind of middle-class living I was used to.

As one community leader cracked when I shared my disbelief at the evolution: "There's still not much need for a college education down here." It was up to me to go with the flow.

Yet, how ironic. I had struggled to get an elusive college sheepskin and immersed myself in the proper climb-the-corporate-ladder route. Yet, I could not get a decent job, while my "no desk, no tie, no meetings" son had propelled himself to the top! Not fair! I had 21 years on him!

In all fairness to this wonderful island, who was I to criticize the Keys culture?

Once I opened my mind and heart, I found myself at peace and smiling a lot. And, I admit, my grandson was a big part of that – such a fun, smart kid. He and his friends would surprise me and stop by after school sometimes. Now that's entertainment!

My spirits were very positive, and it showed. I landed one of my all-time favorite jobs, a contract I accepted focusing on support for a county preschool health campaign to help ensure kids were ready and able to learn. That inspired me to propose naming the new program, "Ready, Set Learn!" I worked my butt off, wrote a successful grant proposal and, with our team, achieved the goal of receiving funding. I never felt so good.

And, my college education did pay off when I landed a part-time teaching position at the area community college. I enjoyed it a lot. I especially liked learning from student discussions.

One night, I brought my grandson along when his dad was on an overnight fishing trip. After class he said to me, "Grandma, it must be hard to be up in front of the classroom. What's it like?"

"Would you like to be the teacher?" I invited. "I'll sit down and be the student, and you come up and stand behind the podium." By now, my "Big" boy was tall enough to peer over it.

So, we traded places. I sat quietly as he looked sternly around the room.

"You're all grounded and have detention!" he shouted. So much for the inspirational instructor!

Dang! Did I sense another young man evolving away from school and toward the ocean?

Like father, like son. Big is already hooked on sportfishing. He's a next-generation Conch and wants to be like his dad and learn everything. Naturally, I brag that he knows how to "swim a bait" and earns tips on charters.

Just Average?

He's unofficially known as "Captain Question."

He's got the bright eyes of his Nordic background and sea burnt brown skin of his Native American heritage. When people ask him about his heritage, though, he innocently says he's "part Gemini."

The ocean and fishing are part of his rightful inheritance.

One day my "boys" and I were heading out to sea, enjoying the sun and salt air, chatting it up on the bridge of the boat. My tanned and handsome son turned to me and said, "Mom, how do you like my office?"

In turn, I said to both of them, "Did I tell you today that I love you?"

"You can never have too many 'I love yous'," Big responded. My heart melted as I gave him a bear hug.

That's when I noticed that sparkle in his eye. *He's* the one who could make it big in movies and commercials! Take a look at his dimpled chin and those sea green eyes! That brown face would fill a big screen to perfection!

Oops! There I go again, pursuing someone else's career instead of my own. Why do I do that? Maybe because I'm afraid that stretching for my own star will mean moving cross country again.

I can't think about that right now. Tomorrow is another day. The second half is gonna go – it's gotta go. I *will* get that KMA membership.

I just wish someone would assure me, "You've got a promising future – and a *nice* behind."

Chapter 2

I'M AS GOOD AS I LOOK

BUTT, HOW I'VE MULTIPLIED!

"Deliciously sinful." For a fleeting time in my life, I believed that compliment!

Reflecting on all my major moves, I realize that my identities are geographically sorted into crates marked, "Minnesota," "California," and "Florida."

Back when I was a young mother in Minnesota, I thought I looked just average at best, considering all the stretch marks. Honestly, it probably didn't matter anyway, because no matter how good a shape I was in, my conservative style of dress seldom showed it off.

My life took a turn when I got my ego kicked by a personal trainer at a gym. This guy actually doubled as a salesman.

It happened when a friend and I decided to spiff up our styles for a long-awaited trip to Las Vegas. As we were shopping for go-go boots, we spotted a sign announcing that "New U" had opened in the mall basement. This was back in the '70s, when exercise was just a part of your everyday life, before it was relegated to "the gym."

We walked downstairs to check it out. The huge guy who greeted us seemed cordial, but his padded muscular hands felt unnaturally cold. The thought that he was "a lunker" flashed across my mind. That's Minnesotan for big scaly fish.

Mr. Lunker toured us around the exercise equipment and then took us back to his office. In a strangely squeaky voice, he complimented us for being in excellent shape for women 'our age.' With his impossibly white teeth glinting in the light, our newest best friend attempted to charm us into the most expensive program, a yearlong commitment.

My real friend and I weren't prepared to write that kind of check, so we politely declined. Lunker appeared to accept that and proceeded to the next level – a six-month membership. At this point, he started relying on guilt. Manufacturing fake concern for our well being, he resolutely emphasized that it was critical to get on an exercise program at 'our age'. Otherwise, we'd soon lapse into looking just exactly like who we were – 30-somethings with kids. We gave him a firm "No," reiterating that we were just checking out the program, though we sincerely appreciated his time.

"Steely" is the only way I can describe Lunker at that point. Somehow, we had unleashed his deepest animosity – though in the case of this particular beast, "animalosity" might be a better fit.

Little by little, the smarminess vanished. His mannerly midwestern facade faded away. The sell became hard and impersonal. His teeth were clenched, and his jaw muscles pulsated. Leaning across the desk, he stared at my friend, a slim 5'6" ballroom dance teacher.

Only his lips moved when he spoke. "You may think you're in decent shape, but your upper body is flabby. You need to lose three inches off each arm."

Though I tried to avoid eye contact with him, he caught my puzzled frown out of the corner of his eye. The target of his dark side shifted to me.

"Don't look at me like *I'm* the one in this room that needs an attitude adjustment, sister. You will never have any fun in Vegas with those hips," he hissed.

By now, my friend and I were more than a little intimidated. It felt like the door was locked. Were we trapped in the concrete cellar of a huge mall with Lunker and his rat'itude?

Inching out of our chairs, we mumbled a hasty "Thanks, anyway," as we reached for the doorknob. He stood up, towering over us. He crossed his arms over his chest with his hands tucked beneath his biceps for optimum bulk. He resorted to shaming us without words by sadly shaking his head at our ugliness and stupidity. We slipped out and hurried up the steps to civilization.

Whew! Now that we were safe, we could laugh. Out of spite, we acted like total juveniles and stopped for hot fudge sundaes. After all, we deserved special treats after such a tongue-lashing!

"Want some extra whipped cream, Hip?" my friend asked.

"You betcha, Arm!" I said, and the nicknames stuck.

What fun is life without hot fudge and a mountain of whipped cream?

I was actually in the best shape of my life ten years later as a 42-year-old lady boomer. I had moved cross country to Southern California to explore the sun and sand of my teen dreams. When I first arrived on the west coast, I was surprised at how "chubby" some of the beach girls were. Overweight by media standards that is, which push a shape so thin no workingwoman can attain it. But, I'll tell you what I really liked about these young ladies. They had glad'itudes! They played volleyball in their bikinis. They had unmatched energy and confidence, and they looked fantastic!

I was not as athletic as they were, but I was slim with impressive biceps. I had taken an extra night job waitressing, which I cheerfully framed as "being paid to exercise." Walking several miles a day combined with swimming and working out with 10-pound weights got the results I craved.

In California, I became the 'hot mama' who looked years younger than her age, rode a Harley and sported a tattoo.

During this buff phase of my life, I received my most memorable compliment. It happened one night when I went to a wild party sporting a see-through blouse and low-cut jeans. A hot guy slowly – very slowly – eyed me up and down and said, "You look deliciously sinful."

Naturally, I accepted his offer for a date.

To my delight, I learned that this gorgeous hunk was into couple's gymnastics. We practiced passionately and soon became mattress champions.

One morning en route from home to my day job, I spontaneously took a detour and dropped by the lovemaster's. He had lowered the bed and was anxious to experiment with sex at odd angles. I sprawled out on the soft blankets. Time lustily flew, and when the afterglow cleared, I realized I was late for work. I called my boss to explain I'd been waylaid on my drive to work.

Trying not to laugh, I put my hand over the receiver and said to the stud, "Get it? Way laid? *Way* laid?"

Believe it or not it actually has an intellectual basis. I can prove it by checking with next line here*Gram's '49*: the first definition of "waylay" is "am-bush." Everything got pulled and twisted in heretofore unheard of pleasurable gyrations. It was indeed a time of fun and bodily abuse.

Though I reflect fondly on those breathtaking workouts, our unbridled enthusiasm was the cause of a nagging sports injury.

It went down the night we were lying in bed at his place watching a travel adventure on TV. A helicopter was touring the Australian outback, when the stud's eyes suddenly lit up.

"Why don't *we* try helicoptering?" he devilishly grinned. "We'll stretch out together, one on top of the other, face to face. Once we're all riled up with my erectile functioning, we'll connect where it counts. The person on top will laterally move clockwise, like the rotors on a chopper – at a vastly reduced speed, of course! The goal is to stay in the groove until we've gone full circle."

"Helicopulating!" I laughed. That we were going to try it was never in doubt. There was just one detail to settle – "Who'll be on top?"

We decided it was more logical for me to be on top in order to put enough pressure on his erect rotor post to keep us attached.

As actively as our imaginations were racing, it only took a couple of minutes for me to climb on his readiness. I began slowly turning. We playfully squeezed and licked each other, rasping, "Contact!" when my hovering positions allowed access to sensitive body parts. By now, the warmth had built to unexplored heights. I was so much in the moment – totally feeling with my body – not thinking with my brain.

That went well until we had rotated half way around, when I opened my eyes. We were now facing each other's lower sides, with his view of my butt's ins and outs totally uncensored. That was vista I needed to block from my mind, so I kicked up speed to move past it. I grabbed at his lower leg for traction, but my hand slipped off his ankle.

BANG! My entire body crashed onto his rigid sex post. A flaming streak of pain coursed through my inner pelvic parts. Obviously, it wasn't good for him, either! Now in pain, his once-rigid post instantaneously slid into softness. The disconnect was an absurd relief for both of us. We called it off for the night.

On future dates we continued to gently bite and poke each other in some awfully tender spots. The final finale came one night when I spontaneously shifted to kiss him just as his teeth began nibbling on my dangling earring.

His jaws clamped tightly together in reaction to my unexpected move, sharply yanking on my defenseless earlobe. Not expecting the sudden sting, I grabbed his head and arched my back higher than a camel's hump.

"Stop it!" I shrieked into his ear. He jerked back and grabbed his ear, his eyes angrily popping out.

That night drove us apart. Playing had become too painful. I blamed him for my sprained back, and he blamed me for his broken eardrum. We "forgot" to call each other.

As a result, I started "laying" around alone. Yes, I mean all by myself. My girth grew stealthily.

Unlike the graceful butterfly hatching from its chrysalis, I emerged from the lusty haze as a mature chick who needs "real woman" bras. This taunting come-on has nothing to do with reality, however, which I largely blame on the dismal selection available in a D cup. What I'd like is a bra that gives support, with two dainty snaps in back, lightly lined for modesty purposes, and comfortable. I don't like my sexuality on display when "my cup runneth over" in uneven bulges. When I do choose to parade my fullness, I'd like it to be adorned in something besides blah beige with sturdy wide straps and seams that cut horizontally across my boobs.

Ironic, isn't it, that the bigger your bra size, the uglier and more uncomfortable the slings get. This, when big breasts cause males to drool more than any other stimuli the world has to offer. I can't avoid the logical conclusion that skinny women design bras. Since they have little heft, they wisely compensate by designing sexy A and B cup bras with colorful frills and padded push-ups.

We abundantly endowed women face yet another predicament when wearing tight sweaters and flimsy blouses. At least, I do. This is something I have never heard about on any daytime talk show or read in any woman's magazine. In fact, I don't think I've ever heard a woman admit this out loud. Okay, deep breath –

One of my tits is bigger than the other. The nipples look out like misaligned headlights – one pale pink "rosebud eye" aims straight forward, but the other drops 20 degrees south of center. Do not get personal and ask which one.

You don't have to admit that the Goddess of Gravity has touched your lovelies if you don't want to. Soon, it won't matter, anyway, because I've thought of a design that would align them without surgery. Let's make nippleless bras for lady boomers with generous nipples. You heard me right!

These trend-setting bras would have a hole centered in the smooth material of each cup where the horizontal line used to be. They would give support while showing off how incredibly sexy we are. Putting the bra on properly would be critical. After the bra is on, you would need to adjust your mammaries so that the pink eyes would peek out the holes. Then, gently coax a bit of the surrounding glory through to ensure a snug fit.

The result? As you know, the shortest distance between two points is a straight line, and rosebuds are no exception. We "full-bodied" women would now welcome a cool breeze as an excuse to shiver and show off our perkiness.

Until that day, though, I need a reality check. The truth is I'm busting out of my bras. In fact, my old jeans don't fit, either. No more bikinis. Sinful clothes are shoved to the back of the closet. Many of my girlfriends have ripened on the vine, as well. One of them told me that when she lies on her side, she can feel her stomach lying next to her. According to a smart-ass mathematician friend, it's not a mystery. "It's input exceeding output." Damn! I hate that kind of logic!

Sadly, the changes in my body shape affect not only how I look, but how I refresh myself, as well. Some personal beautification habits have gone dramatically downhill over the years.

I clearly remember ratting my hair in high school, and the importance of a symmetrical 'do back in the '60s. A stubborn dent in the backside of my head, toward the upper right, was cause for tears. After an hour and a half under a hair dryer, or a sleepless night on brush rollers, the disturbing indentation persisted.

My friend across the block and I would chat miserably for hours about our hair, like the way the flip on the bottom would have definite vertical cracks in it. I used to pretend I had it all under control, advising that if she set her top locks into pin curls, she would get rid of the cracks up there because they were caused by brush rollers. Of course, we were secretly envious of one another's superior hairstyle, but to this day we won't admit it.

But, that was then, and this is now. Somewhere along the way, my hairdo became a hairdon't. Maybe it was when brush rollers went on display at the Smithsonian after the blow dryer revolution.

I know for a fact that by the time I hit my 50s, my primping process ultimately declined so dismally that I forgot to brush my hair one day before going to work! I discovered the oversight when I was rinsing my hands after a morning snack break and happened to catch a glimpse of myself in the mirror. At least that's who I thought it was. The hair on the reflected vision was lumpy in some parts and sticking out in others – all of it sort of separated, rather than waving together. It was kind of scary.

Was I embarrassed? Hell, no! I laughed until my sides hurt. Then I shook my head around like we did when we danced to wild music in the '60s. I smoothed down my hair using my fingers as a comb. Head high, shoulders straight, I walked proudly back to my office.

When the next customer asked, "How are you today?" I cocked one eyebrow and stubbornly responded, "I'm as good as I look!"

Now why didn't I just brush it? Simple. I don't carry a brush. My purse is far too small. I know that you have to expect a small purse to always be full. I realized a long time ago, however, that if I carried a medium-sized purse, it too was stuffed to the brim. Furthermore, a big purse bulged heavily with "unnecessary necessities."

This is proof positive of the old scientific adage that states, "Size doesn't matter, because the junk in your purse rises to its own level." At least with a small purse, you don't have to dig so far to find anything. The small purse habit only exists because as women, we don't always have pockets to carry the essentials. After all, what do we need? Keys, lunch money and some loose change for the newspaper, maybe a wad of tissue if there's room.

My daughter is even more stubborn than I am about the hair-brush-purse triangular relationship. She has exquisite strawberry-blonde hair – long, thick and curly.

But, long, thick and curly are also the characteristics that drive her crazy. I'm talking about a girl who was called "Hippo Hair" in junior high! She literally, some days, could not get a brush through her hair. Somewhere during adolescence she stopped fighting the tangles, ignored her brush and tied it back in a big fat ratty ponytail.

When my daughter was in college, she finally told me about the repeated rude advances that made her steam to the point of blowing. These were the people she didn't know who impulsively stroked her hair when they walked by. She hated being "petted."

She got to the point where she would angrily slap any hand that was on her hair, without even looking at the jerk. Until, one day, she turned around to confront the perpetrator face-to-face and found herself staring at a little old lady with bright, crooked lipstick. "Oh, my, what pretty hair you have," the lady smiled, with red specks smeared on her teeth.

My daughter gritted her teeth, managed a fake smile and a terse, "Thank you."

I had to share this eye-opening information with my friend, Arm, who also had a redheaded daughter. The next time she saw my girl, she asked, "Is it all right if I pet your irresistible hair?" You should have seen the look on my daughter's face! What a crack up!

I actually empathize with my daughter. She came by this hard-to-handle hair honestly. It's a family thing. When I was in grade school, my hair also had its own unruly personality. It was fairly neat when I arrived in the morning but by noon was sprouting in all directions with my bangs flopping in my eyes. After a particularly rowdy recess, my teacher marched me into the hallway and threatened that if I didn't learn to properly "tether back" my unruly hair, she would personally yank all the snarls out.

Her threat may be why, to this day, I obstinately resist carrying a brush.

It's really a moot point, because my hair now falls into place naturally. I've been wearing it the same way for 15-20 years ... short on the top and sides, and long in the back. Each hair has its own elastic memory, and it snaps back into place automatically. I did make a nerve-wracking change last time I got it styled, though. I had the back layered! Whew! It was one giant step for womankind!

Boring, maybe, but consider this shocking statement: even Mohawk haircuts are passé!

Though guys who sport Mohawks today are intending a statement of rebellion, it's comparable to wearing flowers in your hair in the '80s. Both are about a generation gone by. Yet, we all find a comfort level in familiarity, don't we?

Women who graduated from high school in the '40s now invariably wear a short, backcombed, sprayed style, though perhaps a lighter shade of blue than their Mohawk counterparts. Guys from the '50s are still badly imitating that long-gone, full head of hair they felt sexiest in. You know who I'm talking about – the guys who wear a "comb over." They swoop their sparse hair from the top of one ear, continue sparingly over their shiny domes until it settles just above the ear on the other side. Like no one can tell! In a variation on that theme, check out the long-haired hippie guys from the '60s who sport the "bald and bountiful" look – bald on top with a long ponytail down the back – kind of the male version of my outdated style.

Thank goodness for today's trends. Short hair and shaved heads are in, and men with meager locks can proclaim their baldness in an updated, manly way. Some even grow thick droopy mustaches to hide their thinning lips. Here, guys are much more fortunate than women.

Men also have a healthier viewpoint about their extra pounds. When a guy compares his middle-aged body with his youthful one, he often expresses it in terms of, "Gotta get back to my fightin' weight." To a guy, it literally means when he was younger, he could have conquered the professional sports world in any shape if he so desired. He wears his extra weight like a cultural symbol of success and power. Totally unaware of the dust collecting in his belly button, he fondly pats his potbelly as if the star of the team were incubating inside. It's a subtle way of letting you know that he's still trying to decide whether to stay in his sluggish lifestyle or pursue that football career after all. Either way, he's performed.

I can't imagine patting my belly fat as a sign of

success, though I have earned it. I am, however, getting a little annoyed with myself – and society in general – for blaming my starving social life on weight gain and advancing age. I think the stress we women put on ourselves from the pressure to look young and skinny causes worse health problems than a few extra pounds.

Then there's the uselessness of negatively comparing ourselves to others.

We lady boomers were raised in an era when modesty was a virtue. Some of us maintain images of the middle-aged suburban housewives portrayed by the likes of Loretta Young and Donna Reed. But, had we internalized that humble attitude? Had that voice inside us that said we are "just average" been formed in childhood? Were we in the habit of blowing off compliments with responses like, "Gee, I'm glad you like the color of my new blouse, but I actually like the style of yours better."

Check this out: imagine walking down the sidewalk, and seeing yourself reflected in a store window. The tendency is to mutter, "Shit, how did I get so fat and flabby?"

You would never shove that flab'itude on someone you cared about. Instead, you'd be encouraging. So, instead of putting yourself down, how about smiling into the breeze, and thinking something positive.

"I'm only 30 pounds over my fightin' weight. But, I save my sinful clothes, just in case someday ..."

Well, that's progress, but there's still a measure of self-doubt.

Take two.

"The extra weight is good for me. It keeps the wrinkles off my face like natural Botox."

Girl! Stop that.

Take three.

"Well, I may not be that 42-year-old bikini babe,

32

anymore, but I've got great brains and a personality to die for."

Hmmm. Not quite. How about we just leave off *all* the negative body image stuff? How about practicing some *totally positive* self-talk.

Take four.

"I charmed the living daylights out of that young gas station attendant the other day – I sure as hell did. He wanted me."

Let's take positive action steps to lift our spirits. Okay – one, two, three – *ditch* those scales! Throw out that fat'itude! Catch the compliments!

We'll adopt a new motto: "Just say, 'Thank you'."

That simple acknowledgement will show off our new-found confidence. The more self-assured we feel, the easier it will be to praise others. They will respond by just saying, "Thank you." We'll respond with a sincere, "You're welcome!" Just think of the ripple effect as we strut forward!

Positive self-esteem knows no limits, and here's proof.

I'm still breathing hard from a chance encounter I had with one of the most attractive men I've ever met. Was he a hunky romance book cover rip-off? A tanned, smiley guy with gold chains dripping on his hairy gray chest, who imagined himself posing on the bow of a fancy yacht? No! He was actually a highly confident, incredibly interesting, good looking and funny 68-year-old! I didn't think much about him when I first sat down on a bar stool near him.

We started chatting, and before I knew it, I could feel Mother Nature taking over. I found myself sucking in my soft stomach – one of my worst features – and throwing back my shoulders to draw more attention to my soft chest – one of my best features. I have to admit I was very disappointed to know he was on vacation visiting family, and that he had a long-time girlfriend at home. Mind you, this is coming from a saucy 50-something woman who's used to dating guys a lot younger.

My role model for robbing the cradle is a retired friend I loosely refer to as my Bathtub Bitch. She's gorgeous and stays in shape playing tennis, which she does because she enjoys it, not because some stranger in a TV ad guilts her into exercise. I watched her win the annual "Over the Hill and Back" tournament. I admired the way she beat out the other finalist, who was young enough to be her daughter. We met in the clubhouse afterwards for refreshments.

I thought I'd see a lot of high-fiving and hear a rash of spirited game highlights. I was surprised, then, when the focus of the conversation was an earnest discussion on what kind of aspirin or other pain reliever was best for tennis elbow, tennis knee, tennis ankle, tennis toe, etc. Now, these were the best of the best, the most limber of us lady boomers. At first I thought it was silly, but then I realized that, just like much younger athletes, winning is a product of hard work and sacrifice. It's never easy.

I felt my friend's pain and invited her over for a relaxing evening in my rooftop hot tub. I turned the heater on as soon as I got home so the water would be nice and hot by nightfall. She arrived with a bottle of wine, and we sat in the back yard to enjoy the sun setting over the hills. As it got darker, the stars slowly began to light up the sky. We decided it was time to change into our swimsuits and hit the steam.

Trailing our oversized towels behind us, we climbed the outside stairs and stepped onto the deck. We each eagerly threw a leg over the edge of the tub, and gingerly dipped in our toes, anticipating that first hot sting.

Party foul.

Instead of hot, soothing water, it was cold as a cooler of Snow Cones. I scurried around, checking the temperature settings. Yes, I had turned on the heater. No, it wasn't going to work. It was broken. I felt bad. Here she had come over with achy muscles and joints, and I'd inadvertently broken my promise.

We joked about going in the house and hopping into the bathtub. After laughing ourselves silly over that goofy solution, we looked straight at each other and said, "Hell, yeah."

Hot water was no problem there. The real challenge, however, was the old 1920's claw foot tub. It was beautiful to look at, but not more than 4-1/2' long and 2-1/2' wide, deep, with high curved sides.

Fully adorned in our swimsuits, we linked arms and side-by-side backed our butts down into that delicious hot water. We hooked our knees to the top of the tub and dangled our legs over the side. When we needed more wine, we took turns shoving each other out to fetch it.

This gorgeous friend of mine looks pretty much the same in her 60s as she did when I first met her fifteen years before. She became my idol for capturing younger men when she started dating a hunky firefighter. This is a guy so hot that women salivate at the sight of him, uncontrollably chanting, "Oh, baby, come to me." And, guess who he panted after? Yeah. My Bathtub Bitch.

I also know many middle-aged, plus-sized women who are exceptionally sexy. They quit fighting the "Oh – My – God, I can't fit into my size 2 jeans anymore," somewhere back in infancy. They learned to spend their energy being positive.

I, on the other hand, have gotten into a mode of self-imposed isolation. After I left California and moved to Key West, Florida to "help raise my grandson," I began to see myself – and be seen as – a totally different person. I was primarily thought of as the senior member of three generations. My son politely introduced me around the island as "Mom," and the name stuck. Bartenders I would have flirted with and hit up for dates called me, "Mom." One grizzled boat captain exactly my age called me, "Grandma."

"Da Hell!" as we Minnesotans shout while stomping one foot.

Maybe I've been using "Grandma" as a protective barrier from a full, romantic social life. It's akin to my asymmetrically ratted hair in high school. At that time, the dent in the back of my hair, combined with normal teenage zits and big feet, left me feeling inferior to my friends, or just average at best. Now, however, when I look at my graduation picture, I see the lovely young woman I actually was. Someday, when I'm a great grandmother, I hope I'll look back at my younger grandma years with the same perspective.

I think of one popular friend of mine who is smart and full of confidence. Her particular body shape and size don't matter, because she goes with what she's got. As a woman who knows she's deliciously sinful in her own right, she doesn't waste her life by foolishly comparing herself to others.

This talented lady sings at parties and beats guys in dart games at bars. Her first motivation for a fun night out is to please herself. She dyes her hair a warm red and throws on her favorite bright orange feline t-shirt: "I hate being on a leash – me *or* my cat!"

She models her, "I will if I want to" behavior after her fluffy calico cat, sitting on a guy's lap only if she's in the mood.

Stretch. Scratch. Maybe. Maybe not.

I think I'll go out tonight and take her cat'itude with me.

Chapter 3

FUN IS A PERSONAL RESPONSIBILITY

LIVING LIFE AT THE RIGHT ANGLE

*W*hen I'd first moved to California, I was determined to escape my ingrained modesty and beef up my social life.

There was a fun beer joint within walking distance, so I threw on my tennis shoes and hiked over. The joint was practically deserted, except for a guy I didn't know. He was definitely buzzed. But, he wasn't being aggressive, just harmlessly friendly. Even the bartender was leaning on his elbow, bored. So, we started bullshitting and somehow, as it always does in a conversation with me, the talk turned to pro football, my passion.

I tell everyone who asks with unabashed enthusiasm, "I'm excited about the National Football League! I'm a *passionate* Minnesota Viking fan."

I jumped off my bar stool, startling the guys. "Would you believe I schedule my life around games during the season? If I'm flying out of town on vacation, I will be on the ground in front of a TV at kick off. I'll still be there until the 60 minutes of play are over. I painfully suffer the losses and joyously celebrate the wins. Know what I mean?"

I turned my attention to the ESPN sports highlights on the TV behind the bar. "He scores!" I yelled with both arms straight up.

The room was dreadfully quiet. Gradually, I became aware that there were some wide-eyed people hesitating at the door.

"C'mon in!" I smiled. "Help us liven up this joint!"

The two couples pulled up to the bar and ordered.

"We were just talking about passions," I explained. "Mine's football – what are yours?"

"I *looove* hang gliding!" was one woman's enthusiastic reply.

"*Definitely* western movies," her date chipped in.

"*HAM radio* is the *best!*" the other guy insisted.

"Quilting and *estate sales*," his wife threw in.

Even the bartender got into it: "I feel *great* after a long swim, and I *live* for Saturday morning softball league and my volunteer job coaching the juniors."

"*Music* is life," said a longhaired guy who strolled in.

"*Books, books, books!*" his buddy added.

"*Gerbils*," the beer-soaked guy squeaked.

And that ended the barrage with howls of laughter that brought the house down.

Gram's '49 says, "Passion often implies an emotion that stirs one to the depths, a love or hate..."

Ain't it the truth? Wouldn't life be emotionally barren without them – whatever they are? We don't have to understand or embrace others' passions, but shouldn't we respect them?

I actually have a Viking tattoo, a decision that came to me out of the blue one Sunday morning.

I woke up smiling, anticipating the day's game. It was even more exciting than waking up next to a hunky man. Like a thunderclap, I felt the irresistible urge to get a tattoo of the Nordic guy. Sure beats the shit out of getting your boyfriend's name plastered on your forehead. Besides, it's supposed to be permanent. I've been with lots of friends when they've gotten inked. I've never understood the generic tat'itude of, "Let's go to the tattoo shop and look through the book of designs and find something, like Taz."

I couldn't do that. It had to make a meaningful statement. After all, it's a real pain to have a tattoo lasered off.

I've actually had idiots ask me, "You move around a lot – don't you think you'll change teams?" My only response can be, "And they say there are no stupid questions." My tattoo is for eternity. Even "'til death do us part" is not long enough for me and my Nordic guy.

I've always shown off my tat at the drop of a hat.

There was some lively conversation going on at the bar, and I asked if anyone wanted to see my Viking tattoo. It's on my back, left shoulder. I got it there so it would be easy to show off with a low-cut top. That night, though, I had on a t-shirt, so I stood up and had the woman next to me grab the back of the neckline and pull it down.

Everyone smiled in a big way, and admired it as much as anyone could even if they really didn't give a rat's ass about football. I felt pretty proud and was shrugging my shirt back into place when the tipsy guy leaned over me with a smile. "Wanna see *my* tattoo now?"

"Turnabout is fair play," I grinned. He responded with a literal turnabout and then slid off his barstool. He yanked down his pants, bent over and stuck his butt in the air.

"USDA" was tattooed on his ass!

The rest of us laughed until we couldn't breathe. But when Mr. Choice Beef asked me for a date, I decided it was time to move on down the road.

The next stop was crowded and full of locals. I waved at a couple of friends as I scurried to the bathroom. The door was locked, and I could hear a couple of chicks in there, laughing and bullshitting. As casually as possible, I crossed my legs and began humming. But, I knew I was losing the Battle of the Bladder and knocked. They opened the door and invited me in.

One of them was a social friend of mine. Just as I sat down on the toilet, she stood over me, lifted my chin with her hand, gazed softly into my eyes and spoke.

"Want a roll in the hay with me tonight?"

Take me by surprise. "What?"

"Want to get it on?" Yup, I'd heard her right.

Smiling, I said, "Well, I had never thought of you in that way. I thought you had a boyfriend?"

"I do. He knows I'm bi. Besides, you're always so friendly to me. You give me a big hug every time you see me."

"Ah, well, I, uhm ..." I stammered, feeling vulnerable as I tried to finish the job I'd come in for. "That's just how I am. Huggy. To people I like. You're a neat person and fun to hang with."

She was a cool lady, so what the hell, I bought her a beer and we shot some pool. Walking home alone later, I asked myself why I was such a popular girl that night. I looked up in the sky and got my answer. It was a full moon. All in a good night's fun!

But I awoke on one spring Sunday that promised to reek of boredom because football season was now over. As I was suffering from touchdown withdrawal, I realized that a motorcycle ride was just the ticket. Strapping on my custom-painted Viking helmet, I got my motor running and went for a putt. I gained speed, with the cool air and sun hitting my face, and I was transported into a soothing rapt'itude. Damn, it was good to be out and free.

Zooming along, my mood completely, positively changed. This was actually a combination of being in the wind and the ancient stirrings I began to feel as a result of the bike's vibrations. As I felt a silent smile curving my lips, I realized it had been a long time. I'd been hibernating like a bear and was in the mood for company. I made a run to a cozy spot to find some conversation.

Sauntering in, I caught the immediate attention of a rugged guy who eyed me appreciatively as I took off my jacket. I know it was because I looked hot. I had on a tight blue sweater that showed off my bitchy red dyed hair, low-cut boots and rolled-up jeans that emphasized my firm calves.

Feeling unusually self-confident, I approached him and asked enough to learn he was a military veteran, enjoyed the outdoors and was available. In turn, he asked about my purple helmet, where I was from, and other polite questions. I do have to give him credit for being socially competent. He did not get personal and try to guess how much I weighed. Yes, I actually went on a date with one nincompoop who asked me where I tipped the scales. There went that dumb shit's shot at the title.

But, this guy had more savvy. He gave me his full attention, and between the small talk, his eyes signaled his growing interest by occasionally drifting down to my chest, reminding me that I needed to be sure my rosebud eyes were evenly distributed. I excused myself to use the ladies' room.

It was there I discovered I'd forgotten to put on my mascara. Oh, well, take it or leave it. Standing back for an overall assessment, however, I realized that my right breast was bulging out of the bra cup. And, my hair looked like crap. I expected to see it squashed and in need of some fluffing due to "Helmet Hair," which is the opposite of "Hippo Hair." But, the top of my fake red hair was absolutely flat, split right down the middle, with my "platinum blonde," half-inch roots exposed.

I told myself life could be worse – I could have forgotten to pluck a white eyebrow hair. On the positive side, I noticed a zit growing between my forehead wrinkles, a sure sign of lingering youth.

Then I assured myself the handsome guy hadn't noticed any of my imperfections.

I tried like hell to fight off my drab'itude. I told myself if he didn't like me as I was, SCREW him – he wasn't worth it. Besides, I was probably being overly sensitive.

But, honestly, he'd just said, "Hello," to a gorgeous blonde who sauntered in.

Not wanting to face rejection, imaginary or otherwise, I simply left.

To add insult to injury, I got a pipe burn on that little bit of bare calf between my boot and jean cuff.

The least I could do was enjoy the rest of my ride home. I decided to let the vibrations do their thing. Aah, masturbation, the great pacifier.

Enjoying my own company provides only temporary relief, however. Fantasies are a poor substitute for passion that includes slurpy kisses and hugs from someone other than myself.

When an old high school friend was visiting, I confided in her: "I haven't had sex in over two weeks. WAY over two weeks. In fact, it feels like two years. I don't even know if I *want* to try again. Do you realize how long it actually *has* been?" I pouted.

"Cowshit I know?" she responded with a grin. That got a laugh out of me as we began reminiscing about the "malatrokies" we thought were so funny when we were teenagers. That was actually our original slang for "malapropisms," which Gram's '49 teaches us are "blunders in the use of words."

Tired of my whining, she prodded me out to go out for a few cold brews.

"OK," I finally smiled. "Bearshit we go?"

"Flyshit I care?" she laughed.

"It doesn't matter," I responded, continuing our teen talk, "but let's get groin before I change my mind."

"Oil say," she snickered back. And, off we went.

We did have a blast that night. It was especially satisfying to make fun of the prom queens we were so envious of when we were teenagers.

Then, she pointed at me and started laughing hysterically. Between gulps for air, she recalled the time a bunch of us had met for a Saturday night dance at the roller rink. It was in 1963. One of the boys had excitedly shown me a 45 record by a new longhaired English group: "I Want to Hold Your Hand."

I looked at the picture of the band on the jacket and wisely predicted, "With that hair, those 'Beatles' will never make it."

My friend finally let me off the hook, and we began reminiscing about the old albums we had in our closets. We hit on an idea. How about a vinyl party? Records only. No cassette tapes, 8-tracks or CDs. Another eager friend offered to host it at her place the next weekend.

People from 30 to 60 showed up, armed with their favorite collectibles. Some played guitars. Lots of us were singing along, feeling loose. My girlfriend grabbed me for a dance, and we started shaking it up just like we had at that old roller rink.

I really enjoyed myself at the vinyl party. A guy I had a crush on noticed me for the first time, and we shared a lot of music in common. My girlfriend looked at me with a wink and a nod.

We all finally got kicked out as the sun came up. My new admirer grabbed his guitar and hastily wrote his phone number on a napkin, handing it to me as we left.

"Have a good day," he whispered.

"I am," I breathed back.

I wanted to call, though it took awhile for me to feel like putting out the effort to be charming. I have a habit of storing my nicest clothes, saving them for some imaginary special occasion. Even when a noteworthy night does come along, I don't want to take a chance on wrecking them. So, they stay hung up or neatly folded while I slob around in the same old stuff, day after day.

Knowing this about me, my high school friend had followed up on our great vinyl party by sending me a slinky, sexy nightie. She included a note that pronounced: "IT'S TIME". There's nothing like an old friend – a friend you don't have to explain everything to – a friend who knows how to make you smile while taking steps to help you through your problem.

I had not worn that sexy new nightie. Now it got my imagination going, and I actually busted out in hot flashes just thinking about the vinyl guy. Despite my middle-aged hormonal changes, those warm lower stirrings do break through from time to time.

One day, an S-E-X-rated mood absolutely overcame me. It was so intense that I convinced myself to stop procrastinating and try again. The time was ripe to reawaken my comatose vagina for the second half.

Would we? Could we?

I looked through the stash of notes stuffed in a kitchen drawer. I found the napkin with the guitar player's phone number scribbled on it. I had added my own exclamation point to remind me he'd be worth a call. We made dinner plans. I got out a special dress.

So, there I was, at an elegant seafood restaurant with this mighty fine date. The food and wine were great, and the sparkly conversation was filled with sexual innuendo. It seemed only natural the evening's intimate dining experience had strong potential for a lingering, private dessert. I was puzzled, then, when he politely suggested I make a visit to the powder room.

I looked into that damn bathroom mirror and stared stupidly back.

Busted. By a pesky piece of leftover crab embedded between my teeth. It was soft and white, but not the same white as my teeth. Just a shade and texture different enough to be gross and obvious. I dug out the intruding piece of mush with my fingernail. Since my date and I had already had after dinner drinks, I deduced he had been victimized by that white piece of mush for the better part of an hour. I felt a crab'itude scuttle over my enthusiasm.

I should have known better. I'm aware that food tends to get stuck right smack between my two front teeth. Offensive bits of steak and sneaky spices, like pepper, lodge right where there's no graceful way to pick them out. Why hadn't I checked my smile much earlier in the evening?

All the advertisements tell us a confident smile is grounded in clean, white teeth. But to be fair, only toothpaste models have exactly straight, even enamels. Smart-ass me likes to think their teeth are "boring," while my uneven teeth have "personality."

Now, standing in front of that bathroom mirror, my first impulse was to tuck my tail between my legs and emotionally run away. But I steeled myself, instead. I'd come this far and was *not* going to follow my habitual chicken-shit impulses. I was going to set my shoulders back, push my chest out and enjoy this date.

I popped a mint into my mouth and smiled my way back to our table. The vinyl guy looked up at me and broke into a grin. "Are you having as much fun as I am?" he asked.

"Couldn't be better," I flirted back. I grabbed my wine glass off the table and surprised him with a toast: "Your place or mine?"

"Dessert's on me," he quickly responded.

On the drive to his house, I rubbed my hand up and down his thigh. I was going to go "all the way" tonight and not let my doubts overtake my desire.

Walking into his house, he set the car keys on a table and grabbed me for a hug. It felt so good to be in a guy's strong arms, to be kissed firmly by soft lips. I felt my warm body turning hot. "Let's not waste time," I murmured.

We stumbled into his bedroom together, and took off each other's clothes in the dark, seeing only our shadows on the wall as the moonlight shone in through the window. He set me on top of the pillowy comforter and began kissing my neck. I began squeezing his back and butt muscles. Stopping briefly to show affection to my rosebud eyes, his tongue trailed back and forth down to my tummy. I could feel his hardness on my leg.

"Oh, baby," he warmly – though not very originally – panted. But, I didn't care – his breath heated up both the outside and inside of my stomach.

"Oh, yeah – this is the night. You're the one," I cooed.

"Hmmm," he responded as his hot breath surrounded my belly button. He licked above, below and around it in slow, tantalizing circles. Suddenly, he plunged his tongue into the buttonhole. Just as I was grinding my hips in preparation for his next target, he abruptly jerked up.

"What the hell?" he coughed. "What do you have in there?"

"Just ... just a drop of coconut oil..." I stammered. "Why? Don't you like it?"

"Like it?" he barked. "I'm allergic to coconut!"

"Oh, no! I would never...." I began.

"Ptew, ptew" he spat, "It makes me break out." He stood up and turned on the lamp.

Much to my amazement, his lips were already swollen and surrounded with red bumps that were getting larger with every blink of my amazed eyes.

"Will you be all right? What can I do?" I cried.

"I wiw be fine in a widdo wiyo," he managed with his

enlarged tongue. "I have to gwab my anti-awergen thwoat spway." He bounded out of the room.

I was worried. I was mortified. I put my clothes back on, making the educated guess that our intimate night was over.

We rode home in dead silence. He stared stonily down the road. I curled up against the car door.

He was gentleman enough to walk me to the door. "I wiw caw you sometime," were his last words as he walked away. I turned and slouched tearily into my house

I had cleaned my belly button that morning for the first time in years. I'd gingerly adapted to the new growth surrounding the little lifeline cap. My tummy had evolved from flat to flab. Somehow, the extra bulk around the belly button made it smaller. Or, did it just seem smaller? Rather than an open flirty button peeking above my bikini line, there's now a narrow tunnel folded in the rolls under my elastic waistband. Accessibility was a stubborn obstacle to accomplishing the mission.

That demanded a modification of cleaning technique. Whereas a cotton swab used to suffice, now I had to dig around with my fingernail, poking and scraping, periodically checking the nail to see if I got anything. Then, I had to repeat the process at a different angle, attacking another section. And so on, until there was no dirt left, or I needed a break, whichever came first.

After completing this mesmerizing project, I couldn't honestly say I felt more attractive, but I did feel oddly satisfied. As I was getting dressed for my date that evening, I'd spontaneously put that droplet of coconut oil in my belly button, feeling confidently daring.

Now, back home all I could do was shake my head. How could something intended to be such a sexy perk have turned out to be a spitting disaster? When I realized I was mentally berating myself, I shouted, "No!" out loud. "I will *not* do this again! I will *not* push myself down in the dumps. I will *not* curl into a safe shell. I *will* dare the smallest things that put the adventure back in my lifestyle."

Back in the '80s, when I moved thousands of miles from my Minnesota home to California, I arrived with "Miss Conservative USA" emblazoned on my forehead. There were no familiar friends or family to support me, but the benefit of that was that I also had the freedom to change my lifestyle, without justifying why.

I broke out in my forties.

Like some lady boomers before me, that's when I got a motorcycle. What a shitload of fun! Before I go further, let me file the disclaimer that I'm only a fair weather rider. I'm the annoying slow one. Even the flames on my sweatshirt sleeves are upside down, as if I ride fastest backwards. The one time I went down, I was going 5 MPH in a bank parking lot. The day I burned my calf, I was stopped at a gas station.

I'm not like my riding buddy, who was asked: "Do you ride in the rain?"

"No," he curtly replied, "I ride all the time." In fact, he doesn't even own a car.

Speaking from the sidelines, then, I see two basic forks in the motorcycle road. One fork is clearly marked, "Harley" and the other fork says, "the rest." Those who ride foreign brands tend to tell snotty, outdated jokes about how Harleys leak and break down. Harley riders tend to laugh at the feeble "mosquito buzzing" sounds "rice burners" make. Each group feels superior to the other. Oddly, their shared dedication to riding is what separates them.

There is one crossover between the groups – the "RUBS" – rich urban bikers. They are the ones who can simply afford a motorcycle, but don't give a damn about riding as key to their lifestyle. They are the only boring category.

RUBS basically enjoy an occasional summer afternoon's ride to an upscale yuppie roadside bar. Riding their pastel softail models, they sport leathers far beyond what the average rider can afford. The typical RUB has a walk-in closet full of socks and underwear with motorcycle brand names and logos.

Rumor has it a RUB'S bike has 700 miles on it and mostly sits in its exclusive hilltop garage – until a couple of years go by. That's when "the wife," from the vantage point of the leather interior of her perfectly clean SUV, which has never seen a pothole, puts her foot down. Frustrated with the space taken up by the two-wheeled toy in the corner, she snarls, "I suggest you get rid of it!" with all the nag'itude one woman can muster.

Other than the boring RUB, does it really matter what kind of bike a person rides? Well, to be honest, it does matter on occasion. There are those who would never be caught on anything but their own choppers, unless of course, there is no alternative...like when your bike gets stuck.

Just ask an old boyfriend of mine. We'd dropped back into civilization after a kick-ass ride in the canyons. He was on his loud, powerful Harley, and I was on my 250cc buzzing Honda Rebel, "Baby."

Naturally, I was a half block behind when he signaled me to pull over to a hole-in-the-wall diner. By the time he was done locking his bike, I'd parked. We headed inside where we sat by the window to keep an eye on the bikes – at least his. He always said I could leave the key in the ignition and my bike would be safe. After a relaxing hour of munching on appetizers and exchanging insults, we decided to head out.

I slid on my little bike and started her up. Yeah – this

petite black and gold beauty is no plain inanimate "it". Everyone who meets *her* agrees. Oh, Baby!

In the meantime, with Baby running and gas a-wasting, my date was searching through his jacket pockets, his jean pockets, frowning, circling his bike, examining the ground.

"What's up?" I asked, as I strapped on my Viking helmet.

"I can't find the key to my lock," he muttered over his shoulder as he walked back into the diner. He couldn't find it in there, either. Swallowing every bit of pride, he asked me for a ride home to get the spare key. I couldn't believe it. This was a big fella. All meat. I mean a 242-pounder, and I think that was a lightweight lie.

"Uhm," I gulped, "You mean you want to bitch on the back of Baby?" I'll be damned if I was gonna bitch on the back of my own ride!

"Yeah."

"Uh, OK."

He sat on the back, and the bike dropped a few inches. The two of us together weighed more than the bike. I hit the throttle and we wobbled away from the curb. I felt stiff as a board, trying to concentrate while looking casual and confident at the same time. I was scared shitless, if you must know, but too proud to let him take over. Could I balance the heavy load? Hell, yeah – it was just a couple of miles. I could do it.

He directed me to take the back road, as if it were a shortcut. Well, it was my town, too, and I was steaming. I knew he just didn't want anyone riding down the boulevard to see him! I actually thanked him for the suggestion later, though, as he was collecting his spare key. It probably prevented me from getting a ticket for going under the speed limit.

We were laughing so hard about the whole situation,

we could barely stand up. We always gave each other shit. This guy actually had four motorcycles, a mix of American and foreign made. He was a true advocate for the multicultural cause.

There is a serious separation of church and state in the world of motorcycles, though, when it comes to riding enthusiasts like me vs. hard-core bikers. Bikers are wild. Riding is more than a passion. It's a way of life. They work on and sleep with their bikes. They ride in a tradition of worn black leather and loud pipes. They love their Harleys more than their women.

I have to say that loud pipes win out for me every time. That's because I mentally connect loud pipes with vibrations – and you know the rest of that story. Yup, that's why the bad guys get the good girls.

It all makes sense if you reflect on how the American biker subculture evolved. The guys who laid the trail for today's bikers were returning from World War II, happy to be alive after seeing the harsh face of war. Life back in the states was structured and confined. For some, this normalcy was what they had longed for, but for the one percent who could not conform, there was the call to the open road. Those "one percenters" didn't give a damn about how the other 99% rode. They just wanted to keep moving and feel the wind in their faces. Movies like "The Wild Ones," starring Marlon Brando, are made around raunchy, drunken packs of them "taking over" whole towns, just for fun. Some of this is exaggeration, but if it keeps the public at a respectful distance, it's a damn good reputation to enjoy.

Here's the oddest thing, however. For such self-proclaimed independents, bikers are like the rest of us in this way – they conform within their own group. Everyone kind of looks alike, don't you think? If anyone wanted to get away with robbing a bank, it would be a biker during some bike week celebration. Picture that – 25,000 longhaired guys in black t-shirts, with wallets secured to their jean pockets by chains, escaping on motorcycles.

I've come to know that bikers as a family are incredibly loyal. I remember riding up into the mountains to scatter the ashes of a friend who died on the road. There is nothing more respectful than having a hundred bikes trail up the mountainside in your honor.

Some of the guys declare their lasting respect for a fallen brother or sister by wearing a patch on their vests with the name and dates on it. Despite the departing reminder to, "Ride safe," the brutal reality is that some vests have several patches. One friend of mine has a big tattoo on his back as a permanent tribute to a buddy killed in a gnarly high-speed chase. Perhaps these symbols are a combination of respect and fatalism ... after all, as the saying goes, "It's part of the ticket."

No matter what the risks, I do have to state emphatically: bikers have more fun! They are the ultimate creative party animals. Biker chicks were born showing their skin *and* leather. I could never quite bring myself to flash my tits like the other ladies, but one night I did get the nerve to lift my shirt and show off my lacy Marilyn Monroe bra at a local hangout known simply as, "The Place." I'd like to give you a detailed description of how we used to dance intimately with a vertical pole, or about the horizontal action on the pool tables after closing time, but something gets lost in the translation.

Even skirting on the edge, I was included in more good times than any one person deserves. And, to think there was a time when I was afraid to step foot in a joint like that! Sure opened my mind to a tasty alternative lifestyle.

Well, you had to have been there. I wish I were now, but "The Place" is closed.

I was thinking about those days while hurrying home

from a long walk, worried about being late for an appointment. I heard a loud bike crank up in the parking lot of the convenience store across the road. I recognized the one-of-a-kind paint job from around town and walked over.

With my boring adherence to schedules sticking out like a sore thumb, I said, "Excuse me, do you know what time it is?"

The biker looked up at me with his dusty face and replied, "Lady, I don't know what time it is, but I think it's Saturday. Want a ride?"

I thought of all the reasons not to. And then I got on. Fun is a personal responsibility.

Chapter 4

THE DAY MY HYMEN GREW BACK

WHAT ARE THOSE ODDS?

"*HELLO, hello, hello, IS THERE ANYBODY IN THERE? JUST NOD IF YOU CAN HEAR ME. IS THERE ANYONE AT HOME?*"

Pink Floyd's words drifted to the surface of my mind. I was having a dream that my brain was in my vagina. And, though my vagina was feeling "Comfortably Numb," it kept asking the same forlorn questions: "Why can't I perform the function for which I was created? Who did this to me? Where have all the long, luscious rods gone? Why isn't there anybody in here?"

I felt a mixture of emotions for my narrow little one – compassion for her pain, but rage at the perplexing perpetrator who had denied my vagina her inalienable right to the pursuit of happiness.

As I opened my eyes and began to focus on my surroundings, Pink Floyd's haunting, *"HELLO, hello, hello..."* said, *"good bye."* When I saw the sterile green walls, I realized I was actually awakening from surgery – surgery to cut loose the excessive scar tissue from a vaginal hysterectomy that had left me "too tight." The useless hysterectomy that was supposed to relieve a pelvic pain problem worsened since my helicopulating experiment.

Feeling a little dizzy from the anesthesia, I was nevertheless sure I had made the right choice to be knocked out for the procedure. I could have gone with local pain block injections, but that produced a mental image that blew a hole in my pride.

I imagined that my bottom side would be numb but my brain wide-awake. White hats and masks would be hovering over me, the "privacy sheet" across my knees. I could hear the comments flying.

"Damn, she's tighter than the plastic packaging around a new stethoscope."

OR

"Why is she here – is her boyfriend dumb enough to complain?"

OR

Who wants to imagine the word "Oops!" echoing out of my vagina as the surgeon lifts his eyes from the incision site?

Please don't over compensate! I do want to be attractively snug.

Well, so much for the local! I had decided it was lullaby and good night for me.

Before I left for the hospital that morning, I had dutifully showered, packed my socks, and brushed my teeth without swallowing any water per the pre-op instructions. But there was one last, self-imposed prep the hospital knew nothing about.

Following my new mantra – "Fun is a Personal Responsibility"– I felt compelled to get in touch with the last man I had tried to "be with." He had been on top, diligently probing, trying to gain entrée. But, nothing was happening. My vagina was impatiently tapping her toes, so to speak, because the scar tissue surrounding her port o'call formed a blockade that prevented his mast from penetrating.

I, on the other hand, was optimistic. I kept kissing his neck and rubbing his parts, determined to keep him excited during the futile effort to plumb the depths of my being. For a moment, I imagined myself as the star of a new "Cherry Picker" reality show.

In truth, my date was a gentleman. "I thought we were compatible," I think he said. I laid there like a stone, grateful the lights were out.

Remembering that scene just before my surgery had made me wonder if he'd be interested in my scar tissue revelation. He still had no idea *why* our rendezvous failed, and since he's the logical sort, I was quite certain he'd like to know that there's a medical, scientific reason for our "coitus interruptus." I'm not sure if that term has ever been applied to this type of situation, but let's check with *Gram's '49*.

The term "coitus interruptus" is not entered in *Gram's '49*, so we'll have to take it piece by piece. "Coitus" means "coition." "Coition," in turn, is defined as "sexual intercourse." So far so good. The third definition of "interruption" best explains what was happening: "Obstruction of current, progress or motion."

And, there you have it.

So I had asked myself if I should call the frustrated gentleman with the day's surgical schedule. It was awfully early in the morning, and I didn't want to wake him. Or, maybe that was my wishful imagination. Maybe he was already wide awake, bouncing around at that very moment, having a great time with a female whose depths were more accessible.

I left a surprise message on his work phone.

And, someday I'll have to tell him about the unnecessary hysterectomy that resulted in this tight little mess in the first place.

It all started with a constant nasty pain in my lower abdomen. I felt like a perfect "10" on the pain scale.

I tolerated the yucky gastrointestinal probe, MRI, and just about every test available. There were no cysts or obvious indications of disease. There was, however, another possible cause for the pelvic pain.

A gynecologist's exam determined that my uterus had dropped slightly. I inadvertently glanced down at my lap when I heard the news. Seeing my confusion, the doctor went on to explain that just a slight prolepses could cause substantial distress.

The doctor recommended I try inserting a rubber device designed to hold up my droopy organ. It did seem to help a little, but the mysterious pain did not go away.

At my next appointment, the doctor casually suggested a hysterectomy.

Looking me right in the eye, he said, "...no pressure...but think about it."

Somehow, in the absence of any other alternative, it led me to believe that my only real choice was surgery or lifelong pain. Since the intensity of the pain came close to ruining my life, I tearfully decided, "Cut it out!"

In retrospect, surgery was the wrong choice. The pain did not go away. Instead of solving the problem, it created another. My hymen grew back.

Well, not exactly.

What happened was simple. I was stitched up so tightly that I might as well be wearing a chastity belt. I had become a surgical throwback to the Victorian Age.

Of course, there are certainly women for whom a hysterectomy is a life-saving necessity. But, I wonder – how many of us in the "second half" of life have undergone this surgery based on a doctor's wild-ass guess?

My gut reaction would be, "a helluva lot." We lady boomers in our 50s and 60s represent a significant portion of females in the U.S. today. Way too many of us lady boomers are suffering from this mysterious pelvic pain. We become new surgical targets! Since most of us over age 50 are on the downside of having children, our medical track is auto-switched to the hysterectomy as a "cure."

A friend of mine with pelvic pain was pretty much shamed into dispatching her uterus. It was either that, her doctor advised her, or antidepressants. We searched for understanding and concluded that the condescending underlying message was: "If I can't figure it out, lady, it doesn't exist. It's all in your pretty little head." Pat, pat, pat.

After all, "hysterectomy" – the surgical removal of the uterus – and "hysteria," defined in *Gram's '49* as "a wild outbreak of emotionalism," come from the same root meaning – "hystera-," the Greek word for "womb." Ergo, remove the womb, calm down, get over it.

The question that begs to be asked is this: how many guys are told, after suffering years of unidentified testicular distress, "Well, this is a common complaint among men your age, but I can't find a cause for your pain. It must therefore be psychological, and your choices are castration or antidepressants. So, what'll it be, sport?" Pat, pat, pat.

In order to understand this male medical logic, a new organic term is necessary to define a male counterpart for "hystera-" – perhaps "testickle" will suffice? Not to bash men. I am in fact a great admirer – but vive la difference!

To the surgeon's credit, he did caution me that periods of depression among women are common in the aftermath of a hysterectomy. Well, considering this grandmother never planned on having another child, I knew this would not be a problem for me. I just wanted the constant pain alleviated. The emotional downturn, when it did happen, was not caused by the hysterectomy. It was the realization that the pain remained. An exam I had a few months later added to my frustration.

The appointment began in a rocky way when I stepped on the scale. I didn't want to know how much I weighed, so I told the nurse, "I'm going to close my eyes." She smiled, shuffled the scuttle, and announced my weight out loud. A little extra loud, I think, so everyone in the waiting room could hear.

Considering what transpired next, however, that was minor.

After the exam, the doctor smiled and stated that there was no reason for ongoing pain that he could see. Everything was normal for a post-menopausal woman. Then, he uttered in a very satisfied tone, "Your ovaries have shriveled right on schedule."

Eeewwwww! Now, THAT was depressing. It is not something a woman wants to hear! I felt myself growing a steaming bad'itude.

Imagine the outrage of a middle-aged man receiving comparable information. As the doctor is heartily cupping the patient's genital gland remnants, he chortles, "Well, sir, I'm happy to say your testicklectomy was a complete success, and your testickles have been rendered as useless as nature intended."

Wow!

There are also wonderful, fabulous practitioners out there. My older brother – the firstborn, who we call "Bro Born" – and I began reminiscing about our old family doctor. They didn't specialize so exclusively in those days. One afternoon, Bro came home from work to find Mom dizzy and in pain. She was sitting with her head in her hands, trying not to faint, unable to move. He helped her to the car and drove to the doctor's office, where Mom was immediately whisked to an examining room. For over an hour, the doctor and his nurse worked on stabilizing her. The receptionist told everyone else that there was an emergency, and they'd just have to wait.

Since that experience, I always said if I had to wait an hour for the doctor, I'd be a patient patient, because someone needed more immediate help.

This kind doctor and his family lived in our neighborhood. A friend and I always took the kids by his house on Halloween night. They had a long driveway, and we'd wait by the street so the kids could run up by themselves and feel more daring.

"Trick or treat!" they yelled at his door. The doctor himself poked his head out and, recognizing the children, filled their bags with candy.

My friend and I were about to holler, "Hi!" when we had a better idea.

"Free Pap smears!" we yelled.

"If you'll come in and assume the proper position!" he shot back.

Touché! But, that ain't nothin' compared to what happened the next time I went to his office for a Pap.

It was the beginning of April. I had started back to college full time. After a 10-year hiatus, I was ecstatic about being a student, working toward a better future. I never missed class, but one afternoon I had to skip in order to attend my annual physical.

It was the usual procedure, and I was chatting comfortably with the doctor and nurse about family. The nurse took the sample to the lab. After I shared my excitement about being back in school, the doctor wished me well and excused himself. Moments later, he and the nurse returned to the examining room.

"Is it possible you're pregnant?" the doctor asked.

My heart stopped. I stared at my bare toes sticking out from under the paper gown. My life passed before my eyes. All I could think was I'd have to drop out of school.

"I don't think so," I whispered.

"April Fool!" they shouted in unison.

Oh – my – gosh! It was April 1!

I drove right over to my parents' house and told my mom. We laughed until our sides were sore. Sometimes the joke's on you. A medical doctor sees some of the saddest things in life, and if he could keep his sense of humor, then so could we.

Another favorite doctor story revolves around an appointment I had with a specialist. After waiting a half hour, the receptionist apologized and explained that the doctor had been called to the hospital for an emergency consultation. He was expected back any minute. Finally, after more than an hour, she asked me and another patient if we'd like to come back the next afternoon. Thinking about my mom, I uncomplainingly agreed.

Was I ever surprised when flowers were delivered to my home the next morning with a note apologizing for the inconvenience. I about fell over!

During my appointment, I told the doctor that his reputation around town was as one of the top for finding the root of our medical problems. Now, I had to add, "You also have a great heart."

The vast majority of professionals *are* dedicated to excellence. But, just as some medical experts who work on our private parts can search for solutions in all the wrong places, so can those professionals who are paid to get into our heads. Yes, I mean the psychologists, psychiatrists, counselors and shrinks who specialize in our mental health. I think they have usurped the place of family and friends. We are often told nowadays that those closest to us cannot be effective confidants in times of upheaval because at worst, they are at fault and at best, they are not neutral.

Now, I myself have had the benefit of professional counseling, including a prescribed regime that required multiple visits.

My first visit with one psychologist was highlighted by him sliding a little portable desk clock directly into my line of vision while informing me that I had exactly fifty minutes. Pretty cold. Not because there was a time limit. Not because he didn't deserve to get paid. It was because I didn't get the feeling he really cared. He was also very stubborn about trying to direct the conversation his way.

"So you say you are upset because you lost your job."

"Yes, it feels like my security blanket has been wiped out."

"Hmmm...interesting. Security. Did you have a secure childhood?"

"Yes. In fact, I had a happy middle-class childhood."

"What about your mother and father?"

"What about them?"

"Did you feel abused or neglected by them in any way?"

"No – no family's perfect. But we're all human beings, and my parents loved me very much. What does this have to do with my job?"

"What did your family do for a living?"

"My mom was a full-time homemaker and my dad a traveling salesman."

"Perhaps your current employment insecurities are based on having an absentee father."

"A what?"

"A father that wasn't around for you, leaving not only you and your brothers abandoned, but your mother as well."

"My father had to work. Could we get back to talking about my lost job?"

"We are talking about your lost job."

As you can imagine, that was not only my first visit – it was my last. Oddly, he was visibly upset when I said I wasn't coming back. I began to get an inkling of understanding. He really wasn't neutral after all. He needed to drag it out for his own survival. Let's face it – if he stood to make more money every time I came back, well, he had to invite me back often.

Out at dinner one evening, Bro Born and I were talking about this whole concept of counselors who seemed to drum up business by suggesting family childhood problems.

Either we were being loud and loose due to the mighty fine wine, or the young couple sitting next to us was bored and insensitive.

I felt a tap-tap-tap on my arm, and the neighboring gentleman said, "Excuse me, I don't mean to bother you. I'm a psychologist, and I know for a fact that we never try to take the place of friends and family." He was quite tall, sitting up straight and therefore looking down his nose at us. Being testily polite, I asked him where he practiced. "I *don't*," he declared haughtily. "I'm still in grad school."

Well, duh. His training in academic snobbery was obviously going well.

My brother and I barely contained our laughter until they left.

More important than the connection between specific shrink and client is the likelihood that the majority of us, no matter how stalwart on the surface, are hurting at least a teensy weensy bit on the inside. "Baggage" in today's slang. Most of us try to get past our negative experiences by moving forward in a positive way. We choose to use tools suggested by truly caring counselors – and there are a lot of them.

These professionals must be totally frustrated by clients who rely on their problematic histories to excuse ongoing bad behavior, rejecting the notion of personal responsibility.

I had a long-time friend who's a great example. She claimed she couldn't help the thoughtless, offensive remarks that came out of her mouth. She'd been diagnosed in childhood with some babbling disease and therefore just couldn't help it.

"Blab ... blab ... blab ... blab ..."

In truth, she was borderline proud of it, announcing her condition to strangers she cornered at social events. "I babble incessantly," which was in and of itself redundant. Her favorite custom-made pink t-shirt proclaimed, "The *Original* Babblehead Doll!" in shiny silver letters.

After years of trying to understand this babblehead's mindset, I got sick and tired of being stung by her rudeness. Finally, in the midst of one of her critical tirades, I lost my temper. For my own survival, I yelled: "STOP! I AM O-V-E-R Y-O-U!"

Sadly, most people formerly interested in knowing her also walked away. The fact was that the *rest* of the world wasn't going to change. *She* had to. As an adult who had insulted all manner of family and potential friends, she was a perfect candidate for counseling.

Though it can be confusing, nearly all health professionals are truly interested in doing a good job they can feel proud of. Unfortunately, it's that handful of egotistical "pros" we tend to remember, because they have such a memorably negative impact on our lives.

That includes the angry frustration I felt over a couple of slothful environmental health specialists – the arrogant trashmen who left my dumpster in an incredibly unwholesome stink. Literally.

My apartment was situated about thirty feet from a huge trash container. The driver of the truck operated the mechanical arm to empty it. With massive amounts of clanging and thumping the mechanical limb emptied the contents of the bin into the back of the truck. But, there was always some repulsive garbage that fell on the ground around the truck instead of in it. The guy riding shotgun watched. And watched. He watched until the truck left the parking lot and the mess was out of his sight.

I have to give them credit for being consistent. No surprises here – they always left the wayward trash on the ground.

When I complained to my landlord, he was immediately defensive. "No matter how hard I bust my butt for you renters, you're never happy," he whimpered. I swore I saw a fake tear roll down his left cheek as he slowly closed the office door in my face.

I, too, felt like crying, so I got mad instead.

I put in a call to the waste management company. The boss was helpless to improve the service. He claimed that the renters themselves deliberately set the trash next to the can, instead of in it. "Unlike homeowners, renters like you don't give a damn. Go back to your landlord."

Sensing that the excess trash strewing was a losing battle, I moved forcibly to what *really* made me choke – they refused to disinfect the big, smelly can. The putrid mess was an unsanitary breeding ground for flies. I couldn't sit on my patio without being plagued by flies. I couldn't open my door to carry in groceries without the buggers zeroing in. The trash company manager was aggravated by my suggestion that his crew should get out of the truck every week or two and spray the sick can. With obvious impatience, the manager barked, "Their asses are glued to the seat. That's their job." At least, that's how I remember it.

It made me wonder if the guys in the truck had a secret agreement to cut down on the work so they'd each have time to run home and meet his lady for an impassioned "come together nooner." What else could it be? Certainly, they were not focusing on a job well done.

I'm not picking on trash men. I also admire the trash guy who services my friend's home. He works by himself in a smaller truck that he has to hop in and out of every five minutes or so to retrieve miscellaneous escapees. He actually cares and goes out of his way to pick up extra stuff, like small tree branches.

I was visiting my friend when I heard the truck rumbling up early one morning. I threw on my old robe and, not having time to brush my teeth, ran enthusiastically out the door to tell the driver that I hoped he was getting paid more than those guys in the cushy truck. As soon as I opened my mouth, he wrinkled his nose and his eyes glazed over. He said, "Thank you, I think," as he made a quick pivot back to the relatively sweet haven of his truck.

Unfortunately, the lowlifes in charge of "my" trash approach their jobs in the opposite way. They didn't even care that "my" maggot-ridden dumpster was ripening into a full-blown health problem. So, I called city code enforcement for support. The rep told me the problem was occurring on private property, and they couldn't do a thing. At the end of the day, I was ignored by the system.

It was not the responsibility of the trash men or the landlord or even the health department. It was nobody's responsibility.

Of course, it became *mine*, because it was *my* health that was affected.

I was pissed – ready to scratch and claw. Obviously, I needed to convert my negative mad'itude into something more constructive.

After another sleepless night hallucinating about ferocious flies, I quit wasting my time and energy trying to get the services I had paid for. I finally decided to hold my nose and dump a gallon of bleach into "my" industrial trashcan every week. It would have to suffice until I could move, because at least the stench was under control. And – I hope all you bottle fly advocates will remain calm – the offending winged insects were knocked cold.

A friend and I were sipping margaritas on my fly-free

patio one evening, damn near worn out from a long bitch session about all these woes. We finally agreed that sometimes you just have to take care of what you can and save your major battles for what matters most – before you drive yourself crazy and exhaust all your energies.

That's sensible, don't you think? It's just another way of letting go of control that you never had in the first place.

That distinction is especially important when we reach middle age. It can be a beautiful time of life. With any luck at all, by this stage we have discovered what we won't tolerate, and acquired the wisdom to shrug off what doesn't matter. We have learned to choose our battles more wisely. It is *not* always easy. It *is* better.

Was I going to spend my limited time and energy trying to change the waste management system? Complaining about a misguided shrink? Or, organizing a freedom march for my vagina?

Without a doubt, the health issue I needed to focus on was my womanhood. Even though my ovaries had been forced to shrivel "on schedule" – even though the pelvic pain remained – the oblivious doctor who had operated on my scar tissue had said I was "completely healed."

I knew I was not healed. My divine vagina was lonely as hell, and I needed to find out if I could at least ace a full-out romp in the hay.

Who you gonna call? That patient gentleman – the last man I tried to "be with" when my reborn hymen so rudely coitus interrupted us? Yes, and he was willing to take a stab at it.

That very night, he answered the door with his muscular chest bared. He took my hand and led me to the bedroom. His smoldering look said, "Lay lady lay." My clothes fell off by themselves. We sprawled on the bed together. The sheets were cool. He was hot.

We ran through the obligatory bodily warm-ups as

quickly as possible, eager to get to the meat of the visit. He was on top, diligently probing. I was optimistic. I kept kissing his neck and rubbing his parts, determined to keep him excited during the entire excavation effort. For a moment, I imagined myself as the star of a "Cherry Picker" sequel.

And, once again, it was a futile venture. Damn, that stubborn scar tissue did not budge a centimeter. This chastity belt crap was making me tired. Where was a miracle when I needed one?

I began to wonder if the doctor had deliberately botched the job. Maybe it was revenge for my asking too many pertinent questions about that futile hysterectomy. What was he actually doing, then, during that faux surgery? Trimming his nails with the scalpel, hunched out of sight from the nurses? Or, did he give it his best shot, and just didn't have any talent?

If this incompetence isn't a rallying cry for my vagina, I don't know what is. It's time for an action step!

I'm going to write a letter to a medical journal, suggesting that surgeons learn stitching skills from seamstresses. They also sew up, and cut apart, living organisms. Well, sort of. It may be material and not the skin of humans, but what the hell, the concept is the same.

Seamstresses would be visiting scholars at medical schools. They would demonstrate, while SLOWLY and CAREFULLY explaining each step. "WE - WANT - TO - BE - SURE – YOU – CAN - GET - IT."

First, equipment. Proper-sized needles, strength of threads, elasticity – or not – of "fabric." Does it stretch? Tend to bunch? Does the material return to its original shape? All this, and more, would be addressed. While the lectures could be put on videotape for distance learning, passing the course would have to include hands-on lab work. A "Stitcher's Certificate" would become mandatory for graduation from med school.

AND

Many competent seamstresses would finally get credit for their unique talents and skills.

AND

My afflicted lady boomer sisters and I would never again have obstinate scar tissue ignorantly imposed upon us.

Out of frustrations come action steps. When I separate the wheat from the chaff, I fight for my vagina!

Chapter 5

IT IS WHAT IT IS – OR IS IT?

"ONLY ONCE"

*W*hy do some relationships last a lifetime, while others fall by the wayside early on? How can our perceptions of each other change so intensely? And, what is it that makes us choose one person over another in the first place?

When it comes to finding that irresistible partner, those Internet dating companies totally miss the point. The very point that has kept us alive since we first crawled out of the swamp: attraction is not about common sense.

They ask you a battery of questions: what are your likes, pet peeves and favorite activities? You are handed the results of your pseudo-psycho analysis.

Eureka! You have found it! A 100% match – someone who thinks the same way, who has the same interests, values and beliefs. Someone who's thoughtful and hard working, and who looks great in his picture. Someone who shares your weakness for BBQ ribs.

You meet for dinner, but it's a bust. You don't care if he's the most thoughtful and hard-working male on the planet. He's not your type. You don't laugh at his jokes.

On the other hand, "wrong" answers could have produced a love match. It's that indefinable damn chemistry that does it. Your favorite color is red. His is blue. Who gives a rat's ass? You don't have to have a reason for that first spark.

The real mystery is why the same traits that attract us

to someone can evolve into the very same traits that we can't tolerate.

Let's say you first met your future boyfriend at a community picnic. He was the big hunky guy who slammed down his burger platter when he heard some stranger harassing you. Your new hero who stepped right into the jerk's face and yelled, "Knock it off!" Wow! How could a maiden in distress not be attracted to a knight in shining armor?

As time goes on, however, your boyfriend shows this aggression toward guys you think are just being friendly. Now you're embarrassed, not grateful. He seems more like an overblown "Lunker" trying to dominate everything in his reach.

Or, you think it's really cool that your boyfriend is wild and spontaneous. With a last minute call, he's eager to take you for a moonlit ride in the mountains or talk you into sneaking away from work for a day at the beach.

Five years later, after you're married with children, you're sitting at home extremely pissed off, because he's an hour and a half later than usual. When he comes in, all innocent smiles, he relates to you the fun time he had with his friends after work. A retired employee stopped in to say "Hi," and there was a spontaneous gathering. It was more fun than you could shake a stick at. But, you're not about to tell him you're happy for him, or how great it is that he hooked up with some old friends. No. Now, you hate that trait in your husband.

Or, it could be a trait such as generosity. Being a freewheeling spender is a strength when the dollars are spent "spoiling" you, but a weakness when they're "wasted" on someone else.

You get the idea. It really doesn't matter what the particular personality trait is – it's just that it has two sides. So, can you accept the ways in which the characteristic is expressed – positively and negatively?

Yikes! There oughta be a law to clear up this confusion. Why there is: *There are two sides to every personality coin.*

Nowhere does this principle show itself more clearly than in people with tons of charisma. A lover who, by nature, is exceptionally charming to you is generally very friendly to everyone. He's the life of the party, and you're proud of him.

On the flip side, he may be more responsive to other women than is appropriate when you're not around. He is not necessarily taking them home, but he may give them hope. He enjoys – and needs – a lot of female attention. If he doesn't get it from you, he'll get it somewhere, anywhere, everywhere else, even at the risk of pissing you off.

A male friend of mine is a worst-case example of this principle. He was more than a little needy. On the one hand, the women he dated enjoyed his sensitivity and attention. Plus, they were knocked out by his drop-dead gorgeous looks. On the other hand, he was incredibly possessive and jealous.

Then, he found *the one* who brought out the intense passion that "...stirs one to the depths, a love or hate..." He was head over heels in love. They were engaged.

The problem was that, despite his good looks and obvious charm, he wasn't very self-confident, deep down inside where it counts. He was always suspicious of his fiancée's whereabouts and wanted her to account for every breath in her day. When they had a spat, he thought it was the precursor to doom.

The young woman told him she felt strangled. The more he pulled her in and smothered her, the harder she pushed away to breathe. The inevitable consequence was a huge blowout where they talked about breaking up. They didn't speak to each other for a couple of days. Finally, she called. He was high maintenance, but she loved him.

Unfortunately, during that two-night hiatus, he had gotten plastered at the local bar. He was whining and clinging to a pretty barfly, who finally obliged by taking him to her place for comfort. Well, one thing led to another. Word got around.

His fiancée heard about it. She was outraged and confronted him. "Did you sleep with that woman?"

Looking pathetic and miserable, he replied, "Only once."

"Only once" is a mere ant in the path of life when you're talking about a traffic ticket. It is a genuine precursor to doom when you're talking about a breach of trust.

My friend could not believe it when she broke up with him. After all, he *said* he was sorry. And, besides, it was "*only* once." Ironically, he had all along been accusing *her* of stepping out like *he* did.

A lover who seems less socially competent, on the other hand, may also be extremely loyal. He may not give you as much attention as you'd like. Then again, he isn't going to freak out if you don't call for a day. You feel comfortable, but you start to think you're in a rut.

The other person hasn't changed. Your point of view – your perception – your reality – has. *Perception is reality.*

To validate this law, let's take a "Point of View" quiz. The questions will be modeled after the "5 Ws and H" of professional journalism: Who, What, Why, When, Where and How? They will explore your POV – aka your truth – as you see it.

POV #1: Your husband is taking you out for his idea of the musical event of the year.

He promises you it's a performance you'll both enjoy. Your sister calls, however, and advises you to take your earplugs. As you prepare for your anniversary surprise, you ruminate:

A. Will this be that loud, screeching music he likes?
B. Will it be the music that plays with my deepest emotions?
C. WHO should you believe – hubby or sis?

The correct answer, depending on your perspective, is: *All of the above.*

If the musical event is an opera, the diva's piercing ultra soprano range might not be your husband's idea of loud, screeching music that's cool. He could tolerate it just once a year on your anniversary. On the other hand, it's his anniversary, too. But, that heavy metal band that stirs the depths of his emotions is nothing but unintelligible ear blasting to you.

WHO should you believe? Hubby *and* sis. Then trust your husband to go to a heavy metal concert with his buddies and act like wild beasts down in the 'mosh' pit. A wildebeest is, after all, a kind of gnu, which according to *Gram's '49* is, "Any of a genus *(Connochaetes)* of African antelopes, with an oxlike head, short mane, downward-curved horns, and long tail." Yep, sounds like the guys. You, sis and the gnuettes, meanwhile, will chill in the rented limo and drink fine wine in crystal glasses while on the way to the opera, thank you very much. So, to save your marriage, celebrate your anniversary separately. Always keep in mind that, whatever brand of music is on the CD player, "If it's too loud, you're too old."

POV #2: A bunch of friends are watching the usual Friday night scary movie at a buddy's trailer on the back forty of his parents' farm. As usual, he and his girlfriend get hot and heavy in the dark and retreat to the back room so they can grope alone. The others are thinking:

A. Geez, talk about trailer trash!
B. Rock and roll!
C. WHAT should we do – stay or go?

The correct answer, depending on your perspective, is: *All of the above.*

As it heats up in the back room, there's that first barely perceptible vibration. Then, the whole place starts to shake. Pictures crash off the wall. First-timers to movie night are mortified and start to make excuses about getting home. They better hurry, because we old-timers know what's next. This girlfriend is no typical, "Yes, yes, YES!" woman. She's a cat in heat. A deep-throated eerie yowling creeps in louder and louder from the back.

WHAT should we do? It's hard to laugh hilariously, gut busting, high fiving, all without making a noise. But, we're polite, because we want to enjoy future vicarious-S-E-X-rated experiences. Just for fun, we sneak out to our buddy's truck and put a note on the windshield: "You're going to have to tell your girlfriend to quit that hollering. Ma and I need our sleep. Pa." All in a good night's fun!

POV #3: Checking out your teenager's room late one night, your eyes beheld an eerie sight – helter skelter on the dresser, the floor and the window ledge are old milk glasses and pop bottles with mold growing in them. Your gut reaction is:

A. This is gross, totally unacceptable, why I oughta
B. My, that boy has an interesting mold collection.
C. WHY should I care, anyway.

The correct answer, depending on your perspective, is: *All of the above.*

If you are The Impeccable Mother, that little shit is in

trouble. You are fuming so bad the mold is beginning to boil. Your white gloves feel threatened to the core. If, on the other hand, you are a microbiologist, you may actually want to inspect each glass and bottle independently to check for variety. Whereas others think all mold looks alike, you see distinct shapes and awesome colors. Optionally, you could choose not to invade your teen's private space at all. Let him live in his own mess.

WHY should you care? He'll clean it fast enough when his new girlfriend's on the way over.

POV #4: Coming to a fork in the career path, a confused 30-year-old can worry:

A. Am I in my prime and ready to commit?
B. Am I stuck in a dead-end job?
C. WHEN should I move on?

The correct answer, depending on your perspective, is: *All of the above.*

How old is old? Is age 30 the same for everyone? Heck, no. It depends on the circumstances. If you're a 30-something climbing the corporate ladder, you're a young talent being mentored for management. If you're the same age, but a professional athlete, you're over the hill. Many "older" athletes are given the heave-ho by their teams, solely based on age. More is less. But, these elite talents can still run faster and jump higher than those young upstarts. If it were against the law to know someone's age, they'd have years left to compete and win. That's true for us lady boomers, too. Just when we get to be the best of the best, we have to train some 30-year-old rookie to be our supervisor. It ain't fair.

WHEN should you rookies move on? The sooner the better. In the meantime, we veterans will just bob and weave until we can eke out an early retirement.

POV #5: Retiring early at age 59-1/2, you move to a townhouse and stay home all day, relaxing and reading your favorite books. You ask yourself:

A. Isn't this stress-free life fantastic?
B. How can my spouse think I'm boring?
C. WHERE would we go, anyway?

The correct answer, depending on your perspective, is: *All of the above.*

Maybe you *are* boring. Why would anyone get a kick out of looking at your lazy – yet shapely – ass velcroed to the recliner 24/7? On the other hand, you earned it. The kids are grown, and you can spend your money on spoiling yourself instead of college tuition. You don't have a big yard to rake. You no longer need to maintain that three-bedroom rambler with the rusty old pipes. Unfortunately, since the plumbing in your new townhouse shares a wall with the neighbor's, you can hear him quite clearly in the bathroom every morning. But, there's a period of adjustment that's normal with any major life change.

WHERE would we go, anyway? You oughta kick back and snooze on it.

POV #6: Walking down a country lane one sunny spring day, a bright, shiny bird swoops out of a tree just ahead. You look up and think:

A. What a beauty – I wonder what kind it is?
B. What the hell – where'd that sucker go?
C. HOW should I know what's in that birdbrain's head?

The correct answer, depending on your perspective, is ~ "Drum roll, please" ~ *All of the above.*

If the colorful aviatrix flew by to welcome you to the

woods, you feel happy. Such a chipper greeting from one beautiful little bird! You wish you had your binoculars. On the other hand, if she comes soaring back to dive bomb you with her husband and two best friends, she's communicating something else. You had the stupidity to get close to her nest of eggs. She ain't saying, "C'mon up." Like any protective parent, she's telling you to "Move it – now!"

HOW should you know what's in that birdbrain's head? Take a wild-ass guess and trust your instincts. Protect your eyes and change course. Now, imagine a whole bevy of the birds bursting with mad'flap'itude, lined up, cawing and threatening you. Suddenly, size does matter – and the more of those little peckers there are, the faster you should run. Birds could be the basis for a scary movie.

Now that we have proven that perception is reality, for humans and other critters, let's take some action steps to help us in our relationships.

How about a *Personality Prenuptial Agreement*? It would work like this. While in the early stages of wild and crazy love, each person makes a list of the traits s/he finds irresistibly attractive in the other.

"I really like her spontaneity."

"His generosity is amazing."

"The way we move together in the rack is like being in another world."

"You're damn near perfect."

And, in the typical case of young step families, "I love your kids as if they were my own."

You and your partner agree that you will retrieve your lists once a year, on your anniversary. Alone together, you will read your lists to each other. At best, it's a confirmation of all that is well between you. At the least, you both pause to remind yourselves of the fabulous, wonderful traits you initially appreciated.

If you have the guts, you could also mention just one teeny tiny thing the other person could improve on.

"Honey," you sweetly say, "could you make your kids listen to me? Instead of all of us being part of a healthy, blended family, I feel like we're being jacked around on the chop cycle. I would appreciate it if you could keep them under control while I organize a march for world peace."

One major flaw typically ascribed to us women is that we try to change our men. We increasingly harp on them.

Let's take a look to see if we have begun to resemble the harpies of Greek mythology, who were half human, half birds. They were winged monsters with women's heads and long, hooked claws. "Harpy" is derived from the verb "harp," which *Gram's '49* defines as, "To dwell on or recur to a subject tediously or monotonously ... A rapacious person." I can't imagine anyone wanting to be described as "rapacious," which includes, "excessively grasping or covetous...subsisting on prey ... ravenous ..."

Yikes! We're just trying to help our guys improve themselves. But, are we women strong enough to take it, too? There's that daunting challenge to honesty: *You only see what you want to see.*

"Mirror, mirror on the wall... *I* am the most perfect of them all."

Petty nit picking was unfathomable to an older friend of mine who had suffered some *real* offenses. Her family was Russian upper class. Her son was born in Europe during World War II. They were trapped in Germany with bombs dropping all around them. They were in hiding, but her hungry toddler kept hollering for attention. The kid was probably screaming, "Yo, Mama," in Russian.

It wasn't the crying itself that bothered my friend. It was the fear that they'd be discovered. Her husband and brothers had been killed. In fact, all the men in the family had been murdered, except for her father.

Leaving the dead in unknown graves, they escaped to South Africa. Later, her sister was also killed, but her two nieces fled Germany and safely joined them.

My friend, her father, her son and two nieces became their own family. As time went on, her father passed away and her nieces got married. She and her now-adult son decided to immigrate to the United States.

Her son had grown into a big muscular guy nicknamed, "Bull." He had learned to look at life with a sense of humor. Financially, he did very well for himself and bought a lovely home. The zebra skin rugs and poison pygmy arrows that decorated his house were the talk of the town. In fact, at neighborhood barbecues, kids and adults would clamor to hear again the story of how he got his nickname.

It went like this. He'd been out partying after work with his crew from a South African gold mine. A rugged bunch, they worked hard and played hard. Later, he was speeding home in his jeep when he overshot a sharp turn in the dirt road. As he was skidding out the other side, BAM! He plowed into the ass end of a cow elephant. Thrown completely off balance, her bulging butt smacked down hard on the hood of the jeep. The mad cow began trumpeting her distress. The entire herd slowly gathered around the jeep. The bulls began to push on the jeep, shaking it. They wanted to turn it upside down and kill the enemy.

Hiding on the floor, he kept as quiet as possible, but the smart old bulls weren't fooled. They kept shaking the jeep. He managed to hang onto the jeep as it was going over and was temporarily protected under the overturned tin can. With no choice but to pull out the rifle that had lodged between the seats, he shot at their feet, heart pounding. Finally, they ambled off.

Along came the rest of the crew who had stayed behind to close down the bar. They laughed, slapped him on the back and declared him the biggest bull of the bunch. Did they take the survivor home? Hell, no! This was a story that could not wait. Howling all the way back to town, they woke up the barkeep and all the neighbors, too. Drinks were on the house.

After Bull received his U.S. citizenship, he met a beautiful American woman, and they were married. It wasn't always easy, but they were in love, and each thought that the other was damn near perfect. Perfect, that is, until the bottom sides of those personality coins began flipping up.

Soon, the woman couldn't resist complaining about him. To anyone who would listen. It was about small things at first. Then it got so bad the neighborhood gatherings weren't much fun anymore. Everyone began to avoid the entire family because of her shrill mad'itude. Worse, when the neighbors would not listen to her, she gave her mother-in-law an earful. The complaints began to build one on top of the other until the big guy was full of unforgivable flaws.

"Do you know what your son had the nerve to tell me? He likes blue best. All along, he led me to believe red was his favorite color. Woe is me! What have I done to deserve this?"

As the litany of complaints grew louder, the hysterical harpy was bitterly interrupted. Her mother-in-law was seething: she had lost her own husband and ancestral home to war. She would love to trade places and deal with the petty differences of daily living.

She broke in and demanded, "Does he go to work every day? Does he come home at night? What *more* do you want?"

The final straw that broke the marriage's back was

when Harpy began complaining to Bull about his mother. She was jealous of the closeness between this mother and son, these two who had fiercely protected each other, fought for survival and won.

Instead of appreciating this special bond, Harpy began to criticize it. She thought they were secretive. Started calling her husband a "mama's boy." She tried to make her husband ashamed of his relationship with his mother. Bull saw right through it. No attitude adjustment on this planet could save their marriage now. He said, "SCREW you," and gave her the house just to get rid of her. She was ranting at him as he drove away.

In fact, Harpy never stopped.

Holding onto resentment is like swallowing poison and waiting for the other person to die. She ended up screwing herself.

Bull, on the other hand, was not by nature a complainer. He had no regrets, and he had peace.

Eventually, the neighbors found out about the divorce, began calling Bull and coming around again. His new apartment became the center of all that is good about old friends. Sometimes, his mother would join them, and more than one story began with, "Remember when...?"

And, of course, "Bull, tell my cousin how you got your nickname."

I don't know if Bull and Harpy had a Personality Prenuptial Agreement. But I am sure that, like most of us, they entered their relationship with high hopes.

How *do* long-term marriages survive? Is it because each person is perfect, and there's never a skirmish? Is it because they're in a rut and just don't care?

Hmmm, let's give it some thought. It's definitely got to be harder to charm one person for life than a different date each week. And everyone gets pissed, no matter how much you care: *Conflict is inevitable – it's how you handle it.*

Take my friend's parents. They bickered constantly. Bicker is, "...petulant quarreling." It felt like they were always on each other's asses. It made our visits tense. But then, I had to step back and think. They never really insulted one another, which is described in *Gram's '49* as: "To treat with insolence...attack suddenly ... Gross indignity offered to another; an insulting speech or act; an affront ... That which produces injury."

They had been married 43 years. They never had big blowouts. They just wrangled respectfully. I thought, wow, there's something to learn there. I'm divorced. I need to pay attention.

Maybe, I thought, the difference between their generation and ours is the expectation that underlies our vows. They got married with the idea that they'd be together when the sun set on the horizon. Therefore, when they got into fights, their focus was to *resolve* the issue and move forward together.

Today, the comforting thought that, "I can get a divorce anytime," hovers in the background as a safety net. We seem to choose between two extremes – relentless venting or destructive avoidance.

Have you ever been upset with someone – it could be for coming in late or not taking care of business or whatever – the exact trespass doesn't matter – but your hurt or anger lingers because you're too chickenshit to say anything about it? Instead, you let it build until you lose control.

Or, you tell everyone but the person who needs to know.

You're mad at your neighbor. You bitch about it to your husband. Your damn neighbor doesn't change a thing.

You're mad at your husband. You bitch about it to your co-worker. Your damn husband doesn't change a thing.

You're mad at your co-worker. You bitch about it to your neighbor. Your damn co-worker doesn't change a thing.

It can circle around, ad nauseam...

Why do we talk about our disagreements to anyone except the real culprit? Because it has a kind of a narcotizing effect. "Narcotize," according to *Gram's '49* in the sense that we figuratively, "...soothe into unconsciousness." We mistake *talking* about it for *doing* something about it. We trick ourselves into thinking that we took action steps.

But, in truth, we often stay upset and let it build to the point where we blow up. We holler at our partner, "You did it again! You came home from work tonight and left your dirty clothes on the bedroom floor. Who do you think I am, the maid?"

Your surprised partner snaps, "Excuse *me*? I am *so* sorry, but you never said anything before. How would I know? Who do you think *I* am, a mind reader?"

You had a right to be angry. But the other person had a right to know that you're pissed off. After the first or second offense, it was your responsibility to send out a respectful request: "Honey, I would appreciate it if you would pick up after yourself when you're in the bathroom. I'm as busy as everyone else in this household, and we each need to take care of our own stuff."

You realize that, just once in awhile, your husband is wiser than you. By trying to keep the peace on the outside, you were waging war on the inside, which resulted in unintentionally sabotaging any possibility for a productive truce.

Instead, it's time to take positive steps to exorcise the hurt or anger. "Exorcise," says *Gram's '49*, means "To expel or drive off...an evil spirit..." Okay, what's on your mind? One, two, three – kick! Out with the anger and frustration.

One happily married friend of mine – I have to admit, she met her husband through a dating service – said one key to their successful marriage is a pact they made: "Let out the steam before the teapot boils over."

No one can read your mind – let it out, let it go.

Even then, there's a catch. How do you distinguish between nagging about every little irritation vs. respectfully confronting the important things? Can we recognize where a given trespass falls on the "only once" continuum? As we move through the second half of our lives, do we lady boomers get more decisive about what we can't put up with yet more tolerant of others' unique personality traits?

It's related to picking your fights. You make hard decisions and all the rest is crap.

Too bad we don't learn these tough lessons earlier in life. It's all summed up in that ancient universal observation, "'Tis a pity youth is wasted on the first half."

Chapter 6

TMI! TOO MUCH INFORMATION!

GOSSIP PROGRESSES GEOMETRICALLY

*I*f you had it to do over, is there one true love you would do it differently with? Recapture the one love of your life you let get away?

It's not that you can't love lots of people, or appreciate each for what he's worth. But, in your dreams, and sometimes your daily thoughts, is there one who stands out? A lost love who lingers in your thoughts, no matter how you try to redirect them? A man who stands the test of time when all others have faded? The one who, be it for better timing or a slightly different situation, you might be with now?

My most memorable man was the guy I went steady with in college. He had all the qualities I liked: tall, strong, handsome, athletic, smart, funny, straightforward, steadfast and loyal. Alone together, we were in another world.

Being with him was where I first learned to love football. He was a star running back, and I went to the game every Saturday, never missing a second of play.

The women were always around him, clinging to his bulging biceps. We never had a moment's peace. The pushy fans made me impatient to the point where I was rude to some of them. I didn't like myself for pushing back. That was why, despite my passion for this man, I decided to break it off.

As the years went on, I followed his pro career. He

never got into bar brawls with his teammates. He was never accused of taking drugs. Knowing how the media newsmongers could twist information, he kept his family life out of the public eye.

He made it to the top of his game and changed teams when it suited him. His number was the best-selling jersey wherever he played. As a 30-something, he must have looked around at the elite athletes who hung on until they were labeled "over the hill." He decided, on his own terms, to move into coaching. Today, he heads up one of the winningest teams in history and is a shoo-in for the NFL Hall of Fame.

It was great to see him in person at our college 25th alumni reunion. But any dreams I had about us flying into each other's arms for a personal reunion came to an abrupt halt when he introduced me to his lovely wife. They'd been married over 20 years. In addition to being deeply in love, it was plain to see they really liked each other. Even across the room, their eyes met often, and they stayed connected. They were soul mates.

Could he and I have become soul mates? I should have found out. But, like a dumb shit, I threw him away.

One woman's trash is another woman's treasure.

But, this kind of regret is pointless. You can't go back, dammit.

Unless you go way back.

If I had to do it all over again, in a past life, I'd have known Benjamin Franklin, both intellectually and in the Biblical sense. This was furthered by a 300th birthday celebration an intellectual associate of mine had for Mr. Franklin. He'd provided the wine and required each of us to be prepared to share a favorite story or memorable quote or admirable invention of the patriot's.

Me, I stretched it to an imagined scenario. I often fantasize about having a conversation with Benjamin, which would lead to a passionate tryst, of course. Not necessarily an ongoing affair. Only once would have been an inspiration.

There we are, clanking our tankards in a cozy pub as my tight-waisted dress pushes up my boobs. For his optimum viewing pleasure, I'm wearing the revolutionary Real Woman brassiere I fabricated. It draws my paramour's eyes like hummingbirds to nectar water. Benny is regaling me with stories of his latest invention, a wondrous stove.

"My dear girl, an iron fireplace that could be attached to the chimney would make a dandy new stove."

Wow! The seed of our mutual admiration society has been planted.

The dialogue becomes more and more intimate. Our stimulating social intercourse naturally leads to sloshing our ale and generally acting naughty. I am aroused by his earthy humor. "My lovely, beer is living proof that God loves us and wants us to be happy."

Along with the beginnings of an intellectual erection, I feel my crotch pulsating on the wooden bench. In every sense of the word, as confirmed by *Gram's '49,* we are destined to be "intimate" this fateful night: 1. "... innermost ... hence, very personal, private ..." 2. "... arising from close union, contact, association, acquaintance, investigation ... as intimate friends or knowledge ..." 3. "Having elicit sexual relations with."

Blushing, I reveal the enticing definitions of "intimate" found in *Webster's.* "Are you familiar with that dictionary?" I ask the learned Mr. Franklin.

"My dear girl," he bragged, "Noah Webster himself dedicated his 'Dissertations on the English Language' to me. He has a zeal for preserving the purity of our language, and I hold him in the highest esteem. If his tome describes our exchange as "intimate," then so be it. Shall we retire to a private room upstairs?"

"Go fly a kite," I demurely respond, tantalizing him further. He knows I'm going to come, but he appreciates my coquettishness. We wile the night away, wittily exchanging barbs and teasing each other. Then, without a word, we both know. There is no more waiting.

We stagger up the wooden stairs, playing totally raunchy grab-ass with little pinches and tickles. Sprawling on the lumpy straw-filled bed, Benny demonstrates his notable prowess in the art of lovemaking. He's got great moves for a guy with a power belly. Oh, this is one hot patriot. This is a real man who likes a full-bodied woman. He's caressing my rosebud eyes while whispering steamy patent applications in my ear.

The gasps of pleasure evolve into involuntary growls, and I almost lose my mind. "Don't stop jamin', Ben!" I implore, getting his name backwards, "It's never been like this before!" And, ultimately, I burst out with the one thing that hasn't changed over the centuries – the female victory cry.

"Yes, yes, YES!"

"By George! By George!" he rasps.

Dawn is breaking when I smugly say to myself, "I saw, I conquered, I came."

Lying together in quiet celebration of our complete combustion, we look out the window. Dark clouds are gathering as we hear claps of thunder rolling in from the distance.

"You are electrifying," I swoon. "You hold the key to my heart."

"Electrifying?" he puzzles. "Key?"

At that very moment, a bolt of lightning crashes down from the sky.

A look of shock crosses his face. He jumps out of bed, throws on his clothes and spectacles, and races out the door and down the stairs. As I'm getting dressed, I feel frustrated. I know guys don't need afterplay, but this is downright anticlimactic!

I look out the window. There's Benny, in the middle of the storm, flying a kite. He's either fearless or insane – maybe both. Possibly he's a foolhardy genius about to get himself killed. The scene fades to black as I wake up from my fantasy.

I turn on the light and feel a thrill. The average person really can change the course of history.

After that, I took naps as often as possible, hoping to increase my chances of a future jamin' by Ben. This was critically important to my sanity, because my real sex life was in shambles since I was still having significant problems with my stubborn hymen.

The scar tissue left by that useless hysterectomy had proven a formidable foe. With no post-surgical stretching – medical or recreational – the barrier to freedom had regenerated itself. Limited one-finger access did not bode well for the gyrations of a man with a mission. My vagina was still in bondage.

For now, I would have to pursue my erotic dreams of passionate patriots.

Naps became an obsession with me. I am not a good napper, however, and I had to begin some serious training.

First, I shut off the buzzing in my head in order to focus on the very moment. I enjoy the feeling of the soft pillow on my face, the coolness of the clean sheets. Personally, I have to sleep on my side. No feet or hands over the side of the bed – EVER. There are monsters under there, you know.

I must be covered, and the blanket has to be warm, but not fuzzy. I learned this the hard way when I woke up one day snorting pieces of fuzz that had invaded my nose and throat. Like a cat with its fur, I choked out a human hairball. It took a few minutes to settle back down. Dropping off to sleep again is sometimes delayed just a bit as, one last time, I wipe the drool from the corner of my downside lip and scratch my butt, which honestly never itches until I'm trying to take a nap.

Eventually, the subconscious world envelops me, freeing me to romp through various dreamlands, having trysts with any historical figure that my mind and hormones agree on. Honestly, every time I wake up, I'm surprised it's later.

At work one day, I told my boss about the benefits of naps. Through our professional admiration of each other, we had discovered we had a lot of things in common. We had confided in each other and slowly became friends.

Or, so I thought.

I took a deep breath and shared my most intimate experience with Benny. Instead of a conspiratorial smile, she raised one overly-lined black eyebrow. Much to my chagrin, she looked more than a little disapproving. Her idea of a nap, she firmly explained, was not the basis of a trashy novel, but to free your creative subconscious. I needed to learn to power nap.

My boss counseled me that she took a successful power nap religiously after lunch every day. She insisted it was not a waste of time, because she was thinking while she was efficiently sleeping. She was problem solving, thus multitasking.

It sounded anal to me. My idea of efficiency is picking the crud out of my toenails while seated on the porcelain throne. I thought naps were for resting. But, she was the boss.

"Any professional worth her salt," she lectured, "would donate time over the noon hour to gain her second wind." I hastily agreed to give it a try. She loaned me a book from her professional library: "How to Save Minutes a Day...or

Feel Guilty." The author had made millions off it, and it was my homework for the weekend.

So there I was, the next Monday, back in my office after lunch. I had rushed through a ham sandwich so that I could reserve part of my unpaid lunch hour for the power nap. Then, I had reviewed the work proposal I was having a problem with, thinking it would be the last thing on my mind before I dropped off. My subconscious could come up with a solution while I was power napping. Yeah!

Putting on a warm – but not fuzzy – sweater I'd bought over the weekend, I covered my shoulders and felt secure while curling up on my office loveseat. Now, snug as a bug in a rug, I drifted off.

As luck would have it, that's the day my fantasy love reappears.

Benny comes robustly back into the pub, chess set in hand. He likes me for my mind and challenges me to a game. "I barely know the moves," I hesitate.

"... life is a kind of chess," he explained, "By playing at chess ... we learn ..." He raises an eyebrow, awaiting my response.

His passion is contagious, and I cannot resist. We delve into the stimulating game, with him explaining every move. Our social intercourse naturally leads to sloshing our ale and generally acting naughty. Rubbing each other's legs under the table as each move brings us closer to a checkmate, he ultimately wins the game.

"Is it time to go upstairs?" he invites. I'm on it in a heartbeat.

The naughty boy has brought a bottle of Bordeaux. "Of all the wine in my collection, my dear girl, this full-bodied red reminds me of you."

Pouring us each a glass, he proposes a toast to wine and the elbow. Had the creator placed the elbow "...nearer the hand," he enthused, "the part in advance would have been too short to bring the glass up to the mouth; and if it had been placed nearer the shoulder, that part would have been so long that it would have carried the wine far beyond the mouth. But by the actual situation, we are enabled to drink at our ease, the glass going exactly to the mouth. Let us, then, with glass in hand, adore this benevolent wisdom; – let us adore and drink!"

"Cheers!" I shout, chugging the entire glassful in a very unladylike way. I've never enjoyed a party like this one.

"Are you cock ey'd, my sweet?" Benny asks.

For a moment, I think he's asking about the status of my rosebud eyes. Embarrassed, I glance down at my chest to make sure they are fully aligned. Then, I realize he's actually asking if the spirits are making me happy.

"Yes," I whisper, reclining on the bed, "and *you* make me happy."

"In vino veritas," he nods, "truth is in wine."

With that, he climbs on

It is déjà vu repeating itself again. His male plug slides perfectly in and out of my female outlet. It is electrifying.

I am about to yell, "Touchdown!" but I don't want to take the time to explain the future sports analogy. Instead, I chant, "V-I-C-T-O-R-Y!" with the "Y" ending in an explosive: "Yes, yes, YES!"

A sharp rap-rap-rap on the door awakens me from my dream. Oh, no – it's not the innkeeper – it's my boss. I've fallen off the loveseat and onto the floor.

"What is going *on* in there?" she shouts furiously.

As her key is turning in the lock, I'm trying to stand and button my blouse. That was one kick-ass power nap.

"What is going on in here?" she demands, incredulously staring at my disheveled state.

Gulp. This is not my idea of afterplay.

"Ah, well," I squeak, trying to shake out of my delirious daze. "You see," I stutter, "I, was, I was, you

94

know, power napping to find a creative solution to that proposal I'm stuck on. The one we discussed Friday. As you suggested, I'm dedicating part of my lunch hour to freeing my mind."

"Don't be sarcastic!" she exploded. "A lunchtime nap is not the same as a nooner! You were cheating on this company with that Benjamin Franklin, weren't you?"

With that, she stomped out of the office. That holier-than-thou didn't even have the grace to be embarrassed when she interrupted Benny and me.

Damn, she's harsh. What could I do? Was there anything I could say to salvage my job? Would Human Resources believe it was all her idea? That I was just a puppet in a very bad play?

Since this situation is not directly addressed in the employee manual, and since the boss always wins, I decided to lay low. The boss would crook her finger when she needed me.

I have to give her credit. She did not call me in and harp on me or fire me. Apparently, once she got past her – and my – lack of control over the situation, she decided that this was a funny personal matter and not one for company politics.

Except that she just couldn't resist sharing the hilarious story with the business manager.

I began to get suspicious when this particular manager walked by me with a wink. "Getting enough rest these days?" she smugly asked.

I told myself it was just a pure language coincidence. She really *was* wondering how I was doing.

But, a couple of days later, the maintenance man, who I chatted with only occasionally, made a point to stop by the office and jovially ask, "Everything okay in here? Is that loveseat soft enough?" This was very telling, because it came from a guy who complained he got us managers mixed up because we all looked alike. I began to sweat.

The final straw came when the public relations manager informed me, "We're looking for some exciting, off-the-wall stories to get the media more involved in the work of this agency. But, they've got to be suitable for family viewing. Know what I mean?"

Now, *I* was fuming. I stomped into my boss' office and snarled, "You know, you told me we could trust each other, and now you've gone out of your way to embarrass me. How many people did you tell?"

"Only one," she replied.

There oughta be a law. Why, there is: *Gossip progresses geometrically.*

Word had gotten around the office like a raging wildfire.

As I got ready to blast her, I saw her imperial black eyebrow raise itself in warning. I stopped with the next angry words stuck on my lips.

"I quit!" would only hurt *me*, wouldn't it? Was this indiscreet Ms. Blabber Boss going to change for me? I don't think so! Being the one in charge, she didn't have to. I knew if I fought with her, she was the one who would win. It might have felt good at the moment to tell her to go to Hades, but that would only hurt *me* in the long run. I'd be one of many talented lady boomers searching for a job, struggling to pay bills.

There's no lack of technical skill in the world, it's all about being able to get along. She'd just replace me with someone else she could manipulate. In the meantime, I'd look for a new job, all right. But as long as I worked here, I'd focus on revenge. That unethical excuse for a professional leader better brace herself for some serious backlash.

Leaving her office, I had only one thing on my mind – how could I get back at Blabber Boss without her knowing? What kind of personal tidbit did I have on her that she specifically asked if she could trust me with? There must be some secret that *I* could use to embarrass *her*.

Hmmm, let me think. Oh, yeah, I had the perfect story. She took an extended vacation last year – or so she said. When she came back, she looked rejuvenated and had a lilt to her voice, a blush on her face I'd never seen.

In a confidential moment, she confessed to me she'd had her tits lifted. My eyes inadvertently went to her bustline, but I quickly focused on the doorknob behind her chair. The procedure left her looking great with a glow of renewed self-confidence. She felt like a million bucks, and she deserved to. Her husband loved the new perky titties, too. Laughing, he had hinted, "You've got 25-year-old tits and a 50-year-old ass. How about a trip back next year?" It was all set, and she was looking forward to another uplifting extended "vacation," courtesy of her backside.

Now, that's an irresistible chunk of gossip: "She's got 25-year-old tits and a 50-year-old ass." I patiently waited until the week before I left for a new job.

The first one I told was the maintenance man. He would tell a lot of people. Now, Blabber Boss could take *her* turn at trying to figure out the true meaning behind those double-edged questions. The real beauty of it was that, by the time she understood the betrayal, I'd be Out The Door – OTD, that's the key.

I pulled it off without a hitch. Just before walking out that last day, I had the satisfaction of seeing her scurry down the hallway with her shoulders hunched in embarrassment. I was surprised when my gut reaction was shame for my sharing such incredibly personal information. On the other hand, she'd embarrassed me in an incredibly personal way, and I'd never heard even an admission much less an apology from her.

Just Average?

Passing gossipy rumors or terribly embarrassing tales about co-workers can be professionally demoralizing – especially when you're on the receiving end. It's a relatively easy situation from which to escape, though, compared with the traps even well-meaning friends can snare you in. The ones where they insist on sharing with you information you have no business knowing – and sure as hell don't want to know.

Like the friend of mine I told you about who stepped out on his girlfriend "only once." What I didn't tell you was that I had become close friends with his girlfriend, too, and I heard about the indiscretion before she did.

Grapevine communication travels swiftly, and a mutual acquaintance had called me to pass on the juicy tidbit.

"You know, he cheated on her when they got into their big fight last weekend. The night he went out and got plastered." She paused to see what impact the news would have on me.

"What? I have a hard time believing that. And, frankly, this is information I do not want."

"Well, he did," Miss Know-It-All continued. "With that trashy brunette hussy we know from the bar. The one who hangs around with the both of them, pretending to be a friend. The one they invite to barbeques and fix up on blind dates."

I wanted to slap some duct tape across her big mouth. "Don't tell me anymore. Please STOP!"

"Not only did that hussy screw him behind her back, but it got pretty kinky, too." The messenger of doom was enjoying my misery. "She ..."

My heart plunged as I cut her off. "I don't know how you heard this, but it's none of my business."

"The little tramp told me herself. She likes it when guys pull on her nipple rings with their teeth. She brought him over to her place that night, and they were on the floor. He ..."

I hung up. Oh, the perverse pleasure some people get from punching out shock waves.

The phone rang again a few seconds later. I knew Know-It-All was calling back. I refused to answer. But, she managed to get in the final word in a message.

"You know, I have to say, I think the whole incident was more *his* fault. After all, that barfly doesn't have a boyfriend, and she had an honest crush on him. *He* was the one who was cheating. It only happened once. He blew her off after that, and..."

I dropped the phone and ran to the back yard. TMI! Too Much Information!

How do you spell D-I-L-E-M-M-A? I didn't even want to know, but *Gram's '49* insisted: "A situation involving choice between equally unsatisfactory alternatives.—Syn. See Predicament."

That's what I was in, a pretty serious predicament. What should I do?

The first unsatisfactory alternative was to tell my girlfriend. The problem was, she might react by temporarily "killing the messenger" – me.

Another unsatisfactory alternative was not telling her. That meant our friendship would be irrevocably busted if she later found out I knew but didn't tell her.

On a deeper unsatisfactory alternative level, what if I told her and my lifelong guy friend found out? He'd certainly have the right to dump me. And, *that* would be a crusher.

Several fathoms deeper, who am I to judge? The truth is that we never know what's going on in someone else's relationship. Maybe the last thing she did during the big fight was hit him below the belt by shouting, "You're nothing but a mama's boy!"

Whose information was it, anyway?

What would you do?

I finally talked myself into two unsatisfactory alternatives.

If my girlfriend and guy friend did indeed get back together, I would advise him to confess, because it would be better if she heard it from him than someone else. It's plainly a matter of respect. I'd ask him, "Would you want the fear of discovery constantly hanging over your head? Would you want to know if the situation were reversed?" It's only fundamentally fair that they both be making relationship commitments based on full information.

I also made the decision that there was no point in hurting either one if they stayed split. I'd keep my lips sealed. Like we used to say when we were kids, "Zip, lock, throw away the key."

As life would have it, fate took it out of my shaky hands, and she heard about it from someone else soon after it happened. I suspect Know-It-All took on the joy of telling her, but I didn't want to know it all.

They broke up for good, and I didn't have to be the bad guy.

Even the most honorable of us, however, manage to unlock our mouths at the wrong time. This is especially true when it comes to sharing information with our children.

I'd flown down to Key West to visit my sportfishing son and family to celebrate the birth of their new baby girl. One night, my son and I were out at a locals spot, sharing the indescribable joy of welcoming to the world another healthy Conch. Chest puffed up and smoking a Cuban cigar, my son told every fisherman who walked by, "Yep, the baby's here.

8 pounds, 5 ounces."

"*8 lbs., 5 oz.?" they'd repeat admiringly. "Pretty good*

size, for such a little mother, huh?"

"Yep, it wasn't easy. They had to induce labor. The baby finally took the bait, but it was a long struggle. Landed the kid myself, right in the delivery room," he bragged with a proud dad'itude.

"8 lbs., 5 oz.," they nodded, lighting up their cigars.

"We're bringing the bundle home tomorrow. Then, I'm going down to the boat and put the news over the radio. 8 lbs., 5 oz."

It was pretty amazing. He hadn't told any of the guys whether it was a boy or girl! And, not one of them thought to ask. But, like true fishermen, they got the important info – and 8 lbs., 5 oz. was a baby worth bragging about.

Since we were on the topic of newborns, I decided the time was ripe to tell my son that he was conceived directly upstairs from where we were standing. I smiled and said, "Let's walk up to the second floor and sit on the balcony."

Children can't imagine that their parents ever did anything the slightest bit risqué. Even their births were by Immaculate Conception. But, we only look like we're born yesterday. Once in awhile we have to set them straight, just to have a little perverse fun embarrassing them.

My son and I were sipping on cold ones out in the fresh air, enjoying the celebration and starlit night. I started by telling him they used to rent rooms up there. No, not by the hour. I was never involved in the world's oldest profession. Though, I imagine I coulda been pretty good at it with a little training.

Anyway, the rooms were actually efficiency apartments. He was surprised to know that his dad and I had lived there. We used to sit in that very spot on the balcony thirty-some years before. Except for the chairs and music floating out from the jukebox, it hadn't changed at all.

As I thought back, I got a little wistful, remembering.

A torrid love scene began to emerge from the back of my mind. It was the morning after we had caught that huge hammerhead shark. We'd headed home and, despite being up all night, were too excited to sleep, so we sat on the balcony to relax.

I began reminiscing out loud. It was in the early morning light, and we'd started feeling romantic. My man looked at me. I looked at him. All in all, it was an incredible moment, and nine months later ...

I was snapped out of my reverie by my son's insistent, "Mom. Stop! That's TMI!"

"Sorry, son. I didn't realize I'd been talking out loud." I tried for the wide-eyed innocent look, but it took a few minutes to wipe the smile off my face.

The irony kicked in a few days later, when his friends began telling me they heard he was conceived at the bar ... the same bar where they all hung out and got rowdy. I just smiled and said, "Yeah."

Funny, huh. Same information. Shared with his buddies, it's cool. Shared by Mom, TMI.

Sometimes we've got to give our grandkids the inside scoop on their parents, too. My grandson, Big, had been out of school the week before sick with the flu. He told me he'd projectile vomited all over the bathroom. His dad had been relentlessly teasing him ever since, and Big was thoroughly embarrassed.

At first I was annoyed to hear about it, because we were out for hot fudge sundaes with extra nuts on top, and they suddenly didn't look so appetizing. I saw his frown, though, and decided it wasn't the right time to lecture him about manners.

All of a sudden, a memory flashed across my mind, and I broke out laughing.

"Grandma, do you think this is *funny*?" Big asked indignantly.

"Oh, no, honey. But, I'm going to tell you a secret about your dad. When he was about your age, he got sick. He jumped out of his bed, ran *past* the bathroom and into my room, yelling, 'Mom! Mom! I'm going to throw up!' And, then he puked all over me."

"Like father, like son!" he laughed.

Then I wondered if I had overstepped my boundaries. Should I have kept that information to myself? Would my son feel like his father-knows-best status was tainted?

With a guilty conscience, I asked my grandson if he thought adults told kids grown-up information they should keep to themselves. He looked thoughtful and said, "Sometimes." But, then he added, "Adults are supposed to talk to kids. They get their sense through them."

So, I knew I'd done the right thing.

Beyond sharing questionable information with others, there's the ultimate social trespass – exchanging TMI with *yourself.*

Is anyone else tired of all this business about how we must be losing our minds or on the verge of dementia if we talk out loud to ourselves? It was probably a rumor started by a shrink who wanted to drum up business by telling us it's the result of some childhood family trauma.

Oh, get over it! I am here to propose that talking to yourself is part of nature. It is the way we were created. Only a society trying to control its adults would disrupt this age-old method of problem solving.

Have you ever been ranting to yourself while driving down the freeway or stuck in traffic?

One day, I was so intrigued with my own conversation that I missed my exit. Right at that moment, this guy zoomed around in front of me. He leaned out, with his arm extended and hand waving in a "yap, yap, yap" sort of gesture. I mean, the nerve of some people! Such young men should be arrested for trespassing. I was in the privacy of my own car, listening and responding to myself respectfully. I'd made a promise to myself that I wouldn't spread gossip about the conversation. I wasn't doing anything wrong. In fact, I'd just turned down the radio so I could hear myself better.

So, why in hell was I being chastised for this sane behavior? How come I could possibly be arrested, or even institutionalized?

Once – okay, okay, more than once – I was walking down the street by myself, reviewing a conversation I had with someone earlier in the day. I was going over it by speaking out loud, playing both parts. Feeling quite witty and charming, if you must know.

Along came an unwelcome interruption – a guy who walked around the corner and surprised me. He looked at me strangely, but I quickly recovered by going "La, la, la," so he'd think I was singing a song!

Acting like I'm talking to a pet hamster in my purse is also a great ruse, because talking to pets is acceptable in this culture. Have you ever made some clever maneuver like that? Oh, c'mon, the details may differ, but the basic story is the same – admit it. You may have even used this very recovery tactic. If you haven't, I bet you will now. Far more important, why do we have to pretend?

Why is this kind of communication categorized as a sign of impending insanity? It's not like I was going to gossip about it to anyone else.

Think about it.

When you're a new baby, you giggle and coo, all the while playing with your toes. Does anybody rush you to a shrink? Hell, no! In fact, Mom and Dad smile proudly at one another.

Toddlers chat to themselves while playing with their stuffed animals, or while driving a cool toy truck around. "Zoom! Zoom!" Even an older kid will talk to herself, stuff like, "Where's my jump rope?" while quizzically scratching her head, prowling around outside all alone. Why doesn't that behavior seem odd or strange? I think it's because they're having fun. Could we all agree it is the smart, healthy thing to do?

Self-talk is normal.

Take Granny, for example, the old lady who lives next door. Somehow, we agree that it's all right if the elderly talk out loud to themselves. We think it's fine if she asks herself where she put the broom. Or, if she's in the rocking chair on the porch, all alone, chatting to long-dead Grandpa, possibly even flirting with him. We may even shake our heads good naturedly, sympathetic to her loss, but feeling just a little superior over her way of dealing with it.

Granny, meanwhile, wishes that Grandpa, her soul mate, were alive to talk with. She just pretends she doesn't know we're there. That way she won't have to deal with us ignoramuses. *We're* the ones that need an attitude adjustment. Granny's just rewinding the good old days in her head.

Of course, Granny loves her grandchildren dearly, but her most treasured memories are of Grandpa. Out on the porch by herself, she giggles and blushes as she relives those days when it was just the two of them. The old woman reminisces about their 20s during that small window of time in young adulthood when they were rebellious and free. The feeling of immortality the young have makes her smile.

Granny, in fact, was a wild child. She met Grandpa when he came back from World War II. After a hard-fought battle, he was a one percenter, who found it nearly impossible to fit into everyday civilian life. He bought a used Henderson motorcycle, and that was the only transportation he needed. He was alive and happy to be in the wind. When he met the petite nurse with the huge green eyes, it was love at first sight. "Where have you been, Babe?" he whispered.

He made a bitch pad for the back fender, and the young lovers rode as far and wide as their moods took them. Babe would wind her legs around him and press her sweet spot snugly against his back. She'd wrap her arms around his chest, and they'd silently communicate over the miles. Whenever she shivered and sighed, he'd take his hand off the throttle and squeeze her thigh. It was their private signal, and she knew they'd be pulling over at the next woods to find a hidden patch of grass and make mad, passionate love.

After they settled into a small home in the country, Grandpa got together with some World War II biker buddies who also lived on the edge. They very quietly discussed some business possibilities. It was fully understood any breach of confidentiality would result in the loss of life or limb.

In fact, you could peel back their fingernails, but these no-shit hombres wouldn't betray their brothers. Theirs was a very exclusive club.

But, even if you were privy to their private information – which you would not be – would you *want* responsibility for it?

Let me think about it, *no.*

It was a sexist club, but women were welcomed socially. Granny proudly wore "PROPERTY OF (GRANDPA'S NAME)" stitched on her leather jacket. One of her girlfriends shouted her loyalty by tattooing her man's name in two-inch high letters around her neck. Unfortunately, he dumped her right after he got out of jail.

Club parties were by member invitation only. And, if "fun is a personal responsibility," these bikers were very responsible citizens!

Underneath it all, the members kept a watchful eye on everyone and every move.

Signs posted in the clubhouse clearly stated:

"WHAT HAPPENS HERE STAYS HERE"

That's why the top gossip queens of their generation – *their* Miss Know-It-Alls and Blabber Bosses – were never invited. They knew very little about respect, and if they messed up, the big boys wouldn't take the time to teach them manners. They ran on high octane BAD'itude.

Chapter 7

I'VE BECOME MY MOTHER ... AND MY FATHER

THE TOTAL WOMAN IS GREATER THAN THE SUM OF HER PARTS

It's not just gossipers who get on our nerves, of course. Brothers can be a real pain in the butt.

One day, when I was about nine, my big brother and I were having a fight. We were in the living room when he started making fun of me, as usual.

Grrr! I wasn't going to take it, anymore! I sucked up all my nerve and threw my brush at him! Hit him, too!

Like a guard dog breaking off a leash, he was after me. "Mom! Mom!" I yelled as I flew down the stairs to hide behind her skirts in the laundry room.

Guess what? She was upstairs, in the kitchen at the opposite end of the house. What followed must've been awfully painful, because my memory's blocked.

My brother got thoroughly punished. After that, I pinched him whenever Mom and Dad weren't looking. Then he'd hit me, and I'd scream. They landed on him every time.

Until one day, Mom came around the corner and saw me pinch him first. After that, I was on my own.

Shit flows downhill, and I in turn taught my younger brother some lessons. I gleefully recalled the day I told him his nickel was worth more than my dime, because it was bigger.

"Wanna trade?" I asked.

"Okay," said the trusting little sucker. If you consider a week's allowance was a quarter, a nickel was a lot of money in those days. Now, a half-century later, he claims I cheated him out of millions in interest on that nickel.

I also taught Li'l Bro how to ride a bike. Our house sat atop a long, winding driveway. He got on his bike, and I walked behind, holding it steady. The tires slipped on the gravel, and as he took off, he made me promise I wouldn't let go. "I won't!" I lied.

As he gained traction on the downhill grade, I yelled, "Pedal faster!" He did, and then I let go and shouted, "Look ahead! Don't look down! You'll go where your eyes lead you!"

"Look ahead! Don't look down!" he frantically repeated. "Look ahead! Don't look down!" He made it to the bottom, crossed the road and flew over the ditch, landing in a pile in the neighbor's orchard. I knew I'd be in trouble if he got hurt, so I ran down to check on him. Not only was he okay, he was exhilarated. If "Rocky" had been a movie back then, he'd have shouted the theme song.

When my brothers and I were little kids, we went to a two-room school outside of a small Illinois town, in a friendly neighborhood called Waynewood. A picture of the entire student body of Ingalton School has all of us in it. Bro Born's three grades ahead of me, and Li'l Bro is three grades behind.

The seating arrangement was by grade level. I was in the fourth grade with five other students. We took up a whole row, with the younger children on the left. The kids seated in the desks to our right were fifth through eighth graders. The teacher would take some time every day with each grade. While she was addressing another "class," the rest of us would do our assignments. Though we were all in the same room, the strict teacher kept us in line.

There were always those rogues, though, who thought they could get away with talking when the teacher was writing on the blackboard and couldn't see them. But, the teacher had eyes in the back of her head. One stern warning was all she gave.

The students knew they really messed up when the teacher stopped, turned to the supply shelf and took out a roll of masking tape and scissors. It was the old-fashioned masking tape that had to be moistened to stick. She'd cut off a 4-inch slice and march out to the drinking fountain to wet it. The guilty talker – usually a boy – would duck his head, hoping she'd pass by with the tape. But, she'd walk directly to the culprit and slap it across his mouth. When it dried, you couldn't pry it off.

I was Miss Goody Two Shoes and secretly admired the most rebellious kid. That rogue had the guts to push a pencil through the masking tape to make a hole where his mouth was. He'd poke it and poke it and poke it until the hole was big enough to stick his tongue out of. Then, when the teacher wasn't looking, he'd wag that tongue at her with an irrepressible mute chat'itude. Now, that took guts.

My esteem for the daredevil grew. I began tagging him the most at recess. It got to the point where I had to have more of him, so I worked up the nerve to call and invite him over after school. His phone number was easy to remember because our families shared a party line, and the first four numbers for both were "8069." How's that for destiny?

We sat on the floor together, watching our favorite show on the portable turquoise and white television on the table. But I had a hard time focusing on the dancing Mouseketeers, because I was thinking more about HIM.

That was my first inkling that the bad boys get the good girls. The badder the better. Somehow, he knew that, and so his behavior grew even rowdier at school. Finally, the teacher moved him to the back of the room so he couldn't show off for me. Darn, life ain't fair.

All in all, though, the students were pretty orderly. We

learned to concentrate on our own work while hearing the lessons being taught to other grades. It was an educational gold mine.

The music teacher was one of my favorites. Classical music was her passion, and she opened our minds in very creative ways.

To test our knowledge, she would line up a couple of classes at a time in the small side room. She would lovingly take an LP album out of its sleeve, place it carefully on the record player, and gently set down the needle. I always hoped for my favorite, the "Peer Gynt Suite." After a few seconds of listening, the first person in line had to identify the piece and composer. Then the next student in line got a try.

It was similar to the spelling bee format. As long as you responded correctly, you got to stay in the competition. When you missed, you sat down. Either way, you listened to the music for the whole period.

I used to take a lot of pride in winning more often than my brothers. Sometimes I got carried away with the competition.

I cheated once at Ingalton, though not during a music class. It was on a spelling test. The devil made me do it.

The teacher called out the word "cemetery", and I could not remember how to spell it. Was it C-E-M-E-T-A-R-Y? I wasn't sure. But, my spelling record was perfect to that point, and I refused to miss a word! Bowing my head close to my paper, pencil poised, I shifted my eyes to the right, so I could sneak a peek at my neighbor's paper. Cemetery ended in ERY not ARY! I cheated! I changed it! Once again, I got 100% on my test.

That night, lying sleepless in my dark bedroom, I was stricken with overwhelming guilt. Caving in to my tortured conscience, I walked straight up to the teacher's desk before anyone else arrived the next morning. I confessed.

She listened thoughtfully, and after what seemed like an eternity, THE TEACHER SPOKE.

"I'm glad you told me. I'll forgive you this time, but don't ever do it again."

It was like the Red Sea had parted. I was so relieved, I felt weak. I promised absolute future honesty. I volunteered to clean the blackboard.

My criminal career actually had been launched years before. I committed my first robbery at Timmy & Tommy's Superette. I stole a bag of candy-topped marshmallows and got away clean.

Almost.

I was on the sidewalk, headed home, when a guy unloading a truck by the side of the store demanded, "*You*, there. Why aren't those marshmallows in a grocery bag?"

I froze. I was busted.

Did those jerks let me off with a hand slap? Did they tell me to stay away from the store for two weeks? Did they tell me if I ever did it again, I'd be in real trouble?

Heck, no, they acted like Sergeant Joe Friday from "Dragnet." They gave me tough love and called my parents. Fortunately, my mom answered. Unfortunately, she said my dad would have to know.

Maybe the way the pseudo-law treated me in the marshmallow incident caused my anti-social resentment to build over the years. Maybe I felt righteous about cheating on that spelling test.

Well, my teacher's forgiveness changed all that. I can't describe the release I felt. From that moment on, I was free to walk about in society, confident I was no longer a threat. I grew safely into puberty.

Puberty can be scary, though, and nothing was scarier than the one hour of "Sex Ed" we suffered through at Ingalton. It was limited to the older girls. We had to stay after school for it. Each student had to bring in a signed permission slip from her parents. The drama and anticipation built until we were squirming in our chairs.

The source of our anxiety? A film on menstruation. The boys were outside, peeking in the windows. How embarrassing! At least it was in black and white, and not living color.

Mom said I went home and stubbornly told her, "I'm *not* going to do that."

Well, I damn near didn't. Nature always wins, though. At almost 16 those first red telltale spots showed up in my underwear. Now that I'm post-menopausal, I realize 1 was right not to hurry. By the second half, even if you take away a few months for pregnancies, the average lady boomer has had about 462 periods in her lifetime. Multiply that by about five days each period. Certainly, there must be someone to sue for all that pain and suffering

I'll have to ask my brothers if the boys had any kind of sex ed. But, did it really matter? All the kids off the neighboring farms knew exactly how it happened, anyway. I mean, have you ever seen a stallion mount a mare? Or, a couple of pigs going at it?

The boys and girls weren't always separated, of course. We had a communal health film, which vividly showed the negative consequences of sharing body fluids. It opened with a man walking down the sidewalk. He was obviously on the way home from work, because he was dressed in a suit, tie and hat, carrying a briefcase. Our curiosity was only mildly aroused when a man coming from the other direction spit on the sidewalk.

But, then the first man stepped right on the spit with his polished shoes! The tension built as he walked up to his house and opened the door. *Gross!* He stepped on the carpet with the foul shoe. The truly rotten part happened when a baby crawled across the carpet – right where the dad had stepped with his spitty shoe! Oh, boy, everybody in the class turned white.

To this day, neither my brothers nor I can remember if there was even a narrator, because the visuals were so graphic. Honestly, I wish I could give proper credit to the producer, director and actors. Fifty years later, that message is still burned into my brain – spitting is repulsive.

Our school also had artsy coed activities, such as the annual play. I remember Li'l Bro dressed up as an old man in "The Adventures of Tom Sawyer." He got to sing, *"Scat, scat, scat! Darn that cat. Drat that cat. Scat, scat, scat!"* The outfit he wore was probably the inspiration for his annual Halloween costume. Without fail, he was a "bum," with streaks of "dirt" rubbed on his face from a burnt cork, carrying a stick with a packed handkerchief tied on the end.

I was in the "We are Sunny Sunflowers" chorus.

Out on the playground, all hell broke loose ... though we didn't cuss in those days. We could say "darn" in the school play, but the wisest of us knew it was just a substitute for "damn," so it wasn't generally allowed. Instead of cussing, we flung each other around.

Everyone's favorite was a ride called "the twisters." It was a thick, six-foot metal pole planted vertically in the ground, with a round two-foot disc welded horizontally across the top. The disc had holes in it, from which were hung eight chains. At the bottom of each chain was a three-tiered wooden handle, just the right height to hang on to. We would all grab our handles and run together in a circle, but the real fun was when one of us went for a "ride."

The rider would walk with her twister handle around the outside of the rest of the kids, so that her chain was wrapped over the others. Then, the other seven girls and boys would begin to run, and the person on the ride would float higher and higher into the air. Now, that was flying! The girls would pretend the boys couldn't see their underwear when their dresses flew up.

Who could have predicted that some of our grandchildren would one day attend grade schools where recess was eliminated? Bring line below up here In a handful of towns where modern "educators" claim the kids are too hard to control afterward? They think it's safer to make them stay in and play with computers. Then, send them to health class to learn about the theory of exercise.

When we were little, we survived it all. No kneepads. No helmets.

After school, we'd play baseball at the neighbor's in the warm weather, or fall through thin ice in the swamp on winter afternoons.

We sure had a lot of freedom. But, one rule was strict. When Mom rang the big bell attached to our back porch, she knew we could hear it clear around the neighborhood. It was time to go home.

The one way to really make Mom mad was to worry her. We were always greeted with big hugs and a close look to see if we were all right. The school principal admitted to my mother that she was very apprehensive if Bro Born went home with the slightest curl in his lip. She knew our mother would soon be pulling up to the front door, demanding to know the root of his unhappy day. When it came to her children, our gentle, sensitive mother turned into a roaring feline.

The principal dubbed Mom, "The Tiger of Ingalton School."

Mom was a tiger about school at home, too: "You *will* do your homework right after supper."

Dad was strict about work before play on weekends:

"You *won't* go with your friends – you *won't* get your allowance – until all the leaves are raked. And, piled *right*."

Maybe that good old personal responsibility that our parents crammed down our throats really was the ticket. They were looking out for our best interests – self-confident, successful youth turn into productive working adults.

Ingalton didn't last forever, of course.

Eventually, our idyllic Waynewood life slid into memory. Dad was transferred to Minnesota, where the family settled into a "city."

"Culture shock" is the only way I can express the bewilderment of being transplanted to a junior high where I became a speck in a mass of 700 other hormone-driven eighth graders. It was pretty frightening. In a heartbeat, I had gone from being a big frog in a small pond to a small frog in a big pond.

Finally, one girl started sending me notes during English. She seemed like a reject, herself, but at least it was a wedge into the system. She was smart. Serious. So skinny we called her, "Bony."

While she didn't mind being rail thin, she did begin to wonder if she was ever going to grow boobs like the other girls. On the whole, Bony Nobel was pretty cool, and sometimes we did our homework together.

One day over at her house, I made a point to suck up to her crabby mom, who was usually disagreeable.

"Wow, Mrs. Nobel, your house is sure clean," I gushed. Parents were "Mr." and "Mrs." in those days, and you'd better remember your manners around this tough cookie.

"Why, yes, it is," Mrs. Nobel sternly responded. "I've always kept a tidy house. I have never moved my fragile figurine collection off the coffee table. From the time they could toddle, my kids knew better than to touch anything."

She was sitting ramrod straight on the couch – the Original Impeccable Mother.

It was a kind of creepy. All of the little brats I babysat had to touch everything. Of course, Bony was no spoiled, silly teenager. In fact, she didn't have one funny bone in her bony body. She was actually a very high strung, nervous person. I began to get the picture.

Not knowing I'd just experienced the first step to enlightenment, I related the conversation to my mom. She sighed and said, "There are far too many important things you have to tell kids 'No!' about. Most of them are for their own safety. Just forget the 'No's!' that don't matter and store the breakables."

Whew, I sure lucked out when the babies were handed to the moms!

Comparing my mom with Bony's mother, I realized that their hairstyles reflected their personality differences. Whereas my mom's was clean but casual, Mrs. Nobel's definitely needed an attitude adjustment.

Her hair was short and stiff and must've been Dippety Do-ed and sprayed with shellac. "Shellac," according to Gram's '49, includes such cosmetologically questionable definitions as, "purified lac resin...in varnishes...sealing wax, etc."

"Lac," strangely, is, "A resinous substance secreted by a scale insect *(Tachardia laca)*."

Therefore: stiff hair = insect personality. Mrs. Nobel was no prize.

Decades later, by contrast, we lady boomers sometimes forget to brush our hair before going to work. Speaking from an absolutely neutral standpoint, that must mean we are glowingly "au naturel." Au naturel means, "Naturally; to the life; in the nude."

Hmmm, well, almost. Maybe "in the nude" doesn't fit for work. How about we ask Gram's '49 about a related word: "natural."

Definition number 6.b. of "natural" looks like a match: "Being or found in its native state, ... specif: Not artificial, synthetic, processed, acquired by external means, etc.: as, *natural* rubber ..."

Let's see now ... rubber hair ... maybe not. Keep trying.

This is better: To distinguish natural from synonyms such as, "ingenious, naïve, unsophisticated, artless," natural is clarified as implying "... lack of artificiality, and an ease or spontaneousness suggestive of nature".

Therefore, as I see it: wild hair = suggestive nature babe.

Yes! See how approaching a scientific journey from an unbiased viewpoint can get you to your preconceived destination?

On the downside, it would also make sense that unruly hair means a messy house. While I inherited Mom's outlook on striving for a cheerful, caring household, my housekeeping skills were morose by comparison.

It came back clearly when my daughter was in junior high. On weekends, the house was packed with noisy adolescents spilling stuff all over. Sure, I liked having them there – well, most of the time. Okay, okay – I admit, sometimes I ordered the little devils to go home.

In the middle of the usual Saturday afternoon commotion, I stopped my daughter long enough to ask why she and her friends had to play at our house. After all, the other kids' houses were so much cleaner and bigger. She paused long enough to shout, "Because we have more fun here!" Now, who's going to fight a compliment like that and start cleaning?

You would think it would be a priority to keep a home in order. Well, it is a priority. It's just not one I act on. The fact is that, historically, my place has always been messy whether I'm working two jobs or no jobs outside the home.

The single worst housekeeping chore is sorting through piles of papers.

In fact, my sassy kids sometimes accused me of losing their homework! Once in awhile, they were right, but I had to save face. So, I'd muster up my most authoritative voice to remind them, "If it *isn't* where it *is* supposed to be, then it *is* where it *isn't* supposed to be. Keep looking." They'd roll their eyes, but they knew the discussion was over.

If you were Mrs. Nobel's kid, however, eye rolling was punishable by ex-communication, which was why my junior-high friend and I spent most of our time at *my* house, bugging *my* mom. We two rejects became inseparable.

Our popularity gained rapidly when we were in high school. No, not because we made the dipshit cheerleading squad. Simply put, it was because Bro Born was a hot commodity. He was a big shot graduate with a job and money to burn. He picked us up after school sometimes, revvin' his new Chevelle Super Sport 396, and suddenly all the girls who had snubbed us started calling. Running the cruise loop in their family sedans was not the same as being seen in a muscle car.

Older brothers have some positive lessons to teach. Mandatory for a teenager is how to look cool when a police car pulls up in back of you. We were at a red light in Bro's hot Chevy. He glanced into the rearview mirror without turning his head and muttered, "The cops are behind us."

Not knowing better, I turned around in my seat as far as I could and gawked back at them. I saw my brother's knuckles turn white as he gripped the steering wheel.

Boy, did the shit hit the windshield a couple miles out.

"Don't *ever* look at the cops when they pull up by you," he said with disgust. "They'll think you're trying to hide something."

I felt pretty dorky, but I learned fast. Overnight, I

became too cool to bother acknowledging the boys in blue. My street smarts gave me a leg up on the less mature kids my age.

The summer our parents rented a cabin on Lake George, my brothers and I became celebrities. Everyone who was anyone wanted to be there. No one would be caught dead being dropped off by their parents, so they begged to be the "chosen ones" – the select few who got to ride in the hot '66 Chevy. After giving *them* a dose of the "You're a drag'itude" they'd rejected *us* with when we were longing for acceptance, Bony and I would allow them to crawl into the back seat.

We liked to break them in by taking a test walk around the lake, about five miles. The halfway stop was at a little store where they had giant Pepsis. Twelve ounce bottles! Unheard of! We'd sit and sip for half an hour before moving on.

The last leg around the lake was the worst, since we had to wade waist high through Lily Lagoon. Beautiful to look at, but the bloodsuckers made it torture to walk through. As the leader, Bro Born would go first. He'd dip down to his shoulders and wait five minutes. When he stood up, our city slicker friends could see the little black critters stuck to his body. They'd start freaking out, and we'd secretly enjoy their misery. Making a trek through Lily Lagoon was a prerequisite for joining the "Viking Explorers Club." No membership, no more weekends at the lake.

Once we were back on land, there were softball games to play. One day a little girl from a nearby cabin shyly asked if she could join in. "Sure!" She'd never played, but we were happy to teach her.

We let the girl get a hit and flagged her to second base. Next, Li'l Bro was up, and the slugger slammed the ball across the yard. He was streaking toward second when we realized the little girl hadn't moved. She was totally confused.

"Run home! Run home!" we all screamed at her. She tore away like a bat out of hell, ran to her cabin and never came back. We didn't see her the rest of the summer.

Nights were fun, too, especially when the resort owner opened the boathouse. It was actually a little store with a sheltered area outside where the canoes were stored. Inside was heaven. Candy bars were only a nickel, but Mom said we had to share. Li'l Bro was no longer little. He was taller than I was, and he finally got revenge for the nickel-dime incident. "Bro Sis," he said, with his new-found brat'itude, "from now on, *I'm* taking the biggest half."

I "let" him have it.

An old jukebox played sentimental songs like Eddy Arnold's "Cattle Call." We'd wait impatiently for our favorite part, and wail along off-key.

"Woo, ooh, woo, oo, oo, oo. Woo, oo, woo dup do do do do. Woo, oo, oo, oo, oo, oo. Singin' his cattle call."

The last thing everyone did each night was yell, "Twenty Yard Dash to the Outhouse by Willie Makeit!" Then, we'd scare our friends by telling them to watch out for the monster that hid up in the tree along the path. For middle of the night needs, we had a covered "pee pot" under the bed.

My brothers and I were reminiscing recently, laughing our asses off about those endless summers. Until Li'l Bro reminded us that not every day at the lake was fun. Sometimes it rained. Sometimes it was really buggy.

But some days will always stand out for more important reasons. Like when Cuz came home on military leave.

Li'l Bro remembered it as if it were yesterday. Like so many young men who had no deferments due to educational, marital or social status, he and our cousin had been "eligible" for the Vietnam War Draft of December '69. We all had our ears glued to our radios, holding our breath as the lottery proceeded. We were in disbelief when Cuz's birthday came up #8. An eternity later, my brother's was drawn at #355.

"It's hard to believe, isn't it?" he choked. "Two friends, two lives, one forever changed."

While the rest of us were free to pursue our plans for the future, Cuz put his dream for a business degree on hold; instead, he joined the Navy and learned how to wrench pipes in the boiler room. Others went to war and never came back. Some barely made it back. They were all our heroes, because they did what they had to do.

When Cuz came home on leave the next summer, we all met in Minnesota at a public beach for a wild party. Every time we had a toast, we threw him in the water. Even Mom and Dad nodded approvingly. When a neighbor complained that we were loud enough to wake up the fish, Dad advised him to hop in a boat and go catch one.

Dad was always one for "family first." His ideal vacation in the '50s was to take us all on two-week trips in the Chevy wagon. We'd put the back seat down and roll out the camping gear and supplies. Once the blankets and pillows were on top, my brothers and I piled in.

Mom and Dad didn't even like us to read books on our cross-country excursions. Videos like we have in cars today would have been taboo. They wanted us to talk to them, look out the window and see new things. We played goofy games, where everyone in the family tried to be the first to find all the letters of the alphabet on signs and license plates.

One summer, we drove cross-country to Glacier National Park, where we met Dad's hunting buddies and their families in the northernmost site near the Canadian border.

We pitched the old canvas tent right next to a bear trap. It was a big barrel trap, set for a bear that had been wandering into camps. Dad said it was a safe site, and we believed him.

When I got up the next morning, I thought I could hear some rumbling outside. I had to pee, so I cautiously stepped outside to make my way to the outhouse. Much to my surprise, I was face-to-face with the huge bear that was caught in the trap. I shrieked and tried to make a 180 back inside the tent. But, the furry fella had done a big job just before he went after the bait in the cage. I slipped in a pile of ripe bear shit.

After the rangers came and got him, I threw out my stinky shoes. I talked Mom into driving 60 miles round trip into the nearest town for new ones. Being no dummy, I learned to tiptoe around the woods, looking in every direction before taking a step. It slowed me down, but I kept my tennis shoes clean.

Another time a couple of the older girls in the group were going for a walk, and their mom made them take me along. We had traveled about a mile and waded across a creek, when they sat down on the other side to light up a cigarette. I couldn't believe it! They told me not to tell, and I promised. But, deep inside, I knew their parents weren't their worst nightmare. They were going to hell in a hand basket!

For many years, every time we recalled the bear shit story, Bro Born just had to bring up the time my son went out to feed his dog in a Minnesota ice storm. That husky looked like a white she-wolf. As the kid was approaching the doghouse, he slipped, and his face landed in a pile of steaming fresh dog shit. Now, whenever he's within earshot of anyone who says, "This tastes like shit," my son shakes his head and replies, "No. It does *not.*"

Bro Born just had to clear his throat and tease me, "Shit does flow downhill – like mother, like son."

Well, *that* insult required instant revenge. Li'l Bro and I began recounting the day our big brother graduated from high school.

Both our grandmothers were in town for the celebration. They stayed in the boys' room, while the boys slept in the rec room downstairs.

One of Bro Born's older friends had been in a wedding that night and had drunk a few too many at the reception. He decided to walk over to our house for a late-night congratulations. I'm talking about a guy who's so big he makes the man I bitched on the back of Baby years later look petite.

The house was unlocked, so he let himself in. As usual, he headed through the dark for my brothers' room, tripped and crashed on a bed. He crashed, all right. Right on top of Gram! I heard her say, "What the hell?" Pretty soon they were both freaking out, and he flew out of the house at top speed.

All these years later, he still swears that Gram told him he was handsome.

In your dreams.

We were choking, we were laughing so hard. Thank goodness the big guy hadn't taken his pants off first!

The three of us were reminded of one of our favorite games we played when we were little kids visiting the farm where Dad grew up. We used to run around the front yard after dark in our bright white underwear. We'd wait for car headlights to show and then do leaps and somersaults, hoping they could see us. Boy, were we daring! Grandma got a visit from a neighbor, though. We overheard her say, "I do declare!" And, that was the end of that.

We always did what Grandma said. She had muscles

even Lunker the body builder would envy. Into her 90s, the muscles in her wrists bulged from decades of picking berries and carrying heavy crates around the field and back to the farmhouse. Those tasty fresh berries were then loaded on the 4 a.m. train to the city.

Each of us has a secret fear, though. Grandma had tripped on a crack between the stairs during her first escalator ride. After that, any height she couldn't personally control was out – and, that included those new-fangled passenger planes.

So, when Grandma decided to write the family genealogy, she boarded the Queen Mary and sailed across the pond. Speed wasn't in such high demand back then. Today, we get impatient if it takes thirty seconds for an Internet connection. Grandma and her school buddies used to mail postcards to each other – from the same town.

Mom's mom, aka Gram, had an entirely different philosophy about digging through family history. Her exact words were, "Ancestors, like potatoes, are best left underground."

When our parents needed a night out and Gram came to babysit, life was good. It meant races and treats. Who could make it fastest across the living room and back while holding up one leg? While crawling on your stomach? We took this as seriously as Olympic hopefuls, and Gram would cheer us on. She thought we were all champions, and every meet ended in a tie.

We didn't care, because every prize was the same at the end of the night – a piece of homemade fudge hidden inside a root beer float.

Gram wasn't nuts about ice cream, but she loved stinky Limburger cheese! On Christmas Eve, we followed the Swedish tradition of eating herring, which others might ignorantly refer to as Swedish sushi – or possibly, bait.

You can see that strong, stubborn and stinky are all part of our rightful inheritance.

The three of us then turned to reminiscing about Mom and Dad, who've both been gone a long time. They had their ups and downs, but they were soul mates. Dad went first, and when it was Mom's turn, she was ready. "I want to be with my husband."

As you know, even if you're middle-aged when your parents pass on, you still suffer. You're never ready. When you've lost both parents, you are orphans. Gram's '49 substantiates this. An orphan is "A child bereaved by death of both father and mother...to deprive of parents."

You are always your parents' child.

Though we are orphans, we are blessed. Having children of our own, we understand the worries our parents had about us. We understand why they often just said, "No."

We grew up to be an awfully lot like our mother...and our father.

Mom and Dad would be very happy about the core of love that's been passed up, down and across generations. We are friends with our aunts and uncles. We are friends with our nieces and nephews. We are friends with our own kids. Our kids are friends. We travel to see each other.

Three generations came even closer through tragedies that happened 60 years apart.

I clearly recall November 22, 1963. I was a high school junior, and we had just settled into World History class after lunch. The teacher wrote on the blackboard: "THE PRESIDENT HAS BEEN SHOT."

I thought, "What kind of assignment could he possibly be leading us into?"

Then the teacher slumped down into the chair behind his desk, with his head in his hands. The loudspeakers came on...

I have never forgotten that moment in time – the disbelief that was my first reaction, and the pain that has never gone away.

During President Kennedy's televised funeral, some friends stopped by our house to see if I wanted to go for a ride. My Dad said, "No. You need to stay home and watch this. This is history." He was right.

Our children often retell the stories of where they were on September 11, 2001, and how they felt when they realized the planes that slammed into the World Trade Center were a terrible terrorist attack, not an awful accident. The tragic events of 9-11 help them relate to what we went through over 40 years ago – just as it took the assassination of John F. Kennedy for my generation to understand the horror experienced by our parents when Pearl Harbor was bombed on December 7, 1941. The loss of security, the confusion and the emotions that our three generations experienced 60 years apart are shared among us.

More than these solemn recollections, however, family gatherings focus on the funny memories. Inevitably, someone starts a round of stories behind the shitload of goofy nicknames we've nailed each other with over the years!

Nicknames, like true friendships, evolve over time and not on demand. They are part of a shared history. Like it or not, they usually have a grain of truth. Yeah, they might be a little embarrassing, but you've got to have faith that we tease the people we like and trust.

In fact, we could make up a new party game to jump start the big family reunions, where long-lost relatives don't know who the hell you are, much less know about your life's experiences. Reminiscing through family folklore serves as the ancestral glue.

Alternatively, this game could even be played at employee parties. It would be especially fun for guests who have no clue as to what your real name is, but may be curious why you're known as "Tiger" around the office.

Okay, let's get organized. On the left side of a sheet of paper, list a dozen peoples' given names. On the right, in random order, write a dozen related nicknames. Depending on the popularity of the game and the frequency played, you could hand out preprinted forms.

Then, list random statements that tell how the person earned the nickname. They could be called the "Missing Links." Yeah – The Nickname Game!

This is what mine would look like. I'll describe some people and you guess which nickname belongs to whom and the reason why. Just draw connecting lines, and add the Missing Link. I'll give you one hint, just to make sure your virgin experience is a good one.

THE NICKNAME GAME

Real name	Nickname	Missing Link
Kent	Pyro	?
Paul	Shitsky	?
Gripper	Jewels	?
Captain	Dent	?
Madame Harrington	Shadow	?

Missing Links

ML1: As a kid, this future fisherman slipped on the ice when running out to feed the dog, and his face landed in a pile of steaming dog shit. HINT: shit. A no-brainer.

ML 2: He and a pal wanted to know if it were possible to light a ball of deodorant on fire – it was, and when the gas can exploded, the whole shed burned down.

ML3: He crashed during a bicycle race, and a rock gouged a big hole in his forehead, and after the scab fell off, it left a deep, round scar where the pigment wouldn't grow, but no one teased him until the day he laughed at a mail solicitation with a typo in his name.

ML4: A bold redheaded ancestor, she emigrated here from a war-torn country, became a famous poet who always wore a diamond necklace as a symbol of her success. She commanded, "Treat me with respect – don't you ever call me _____!"

ML5: This is one cool cat who always knew it was better to laze around under the old oak than work up a sweat running around a field chasing a ball.

What's *your* favorite or most embarrassing childhood nickname?

Does it matter? Hell, yeah!

Old friends and family *are* the best. My Bros and I are tight, and we keep alive the memories behind those goofy nicknames. I especially enjoy the stories my brothers tell about their hunting trips with Dad.

Dad went deer hunting with the same bunch of guys for over 40 years. Modest by nature, he'd turn into a stand-up comic in front of his buddies, throwing out dry one-liners like, "Did you know it requires three eyes to thread a needle?" He was the leader and would bring along beer and peppermint schnapps for the whole gang the night before the first hunt. His buddies saluted him with a toast, "To the Captain!"

On the 20th anniversary of Dad's passing, my brothers and I had a three-way phone conversation. We were spread apart, all across the country, busy with our jobs. As with any special event, we agreed on the time and format a few days ahead.

Each of us would have beer and schnapps in hand. Starting with Bro Born, we would take turns telling a favorite story about our family. The storyteller would then propose a toast, "To the Captain!"

Who else but your siblings can you get looped with on the phone while taking turns telling stories – sometimes laughing, sometimes somber. It was a wonderful night reminiscing about our family, here and gone.

It was more than fun. It was memorable, and we all agreed that Mom and Dad are still our greatest champions. Got a problem with the school principal? Talk to your parents. God doesn't answer your prayer? Call on Mom and Dad. No blasphemy intended, Lord – geez, we hope we don't get struck by lightning!

It was suddenly 2-1/2 hours later. How many toasts were lifted? A lot!

If we could say one more thing to Mom and Dad, what would it be? In quiet unison, across the miles, we three raised our glasses in a toast to our folks, the ones whose nicknames mean the most of all:

"To the Captain! And The Tiger of Ingalton School"

Chapter 8

MIDDLE CLASS, MIDDLE AGE

+ *PLUS OR MINUS* -

"Money doesn't buy happiness."
Yeah, right.
There is blatantly false logic in saying the rich have the same problems as we middle-class folks. These "words of wisdom" can only be part of a plot to squash a bourgeoisie rebellion.

Sure, people of any socioeconomic status can be hit with a tragedy. I think I've finally figured out the difference between us and them: money does buy *survival*.

There was a magazine article about some celebrity lady boomers who'd suffered personal tragedies, such as being dumped by their husbands for younger women. Naturally, they were grief stricken, mortified and crushed. The world was teetering on its emotional axis. These high-income ladies were suffering the same human depression we all would under those circumstances. Getting over it was tough.

The interviewer's focus was: "How did you move on?"

Some of these shattered hearts fled to their country homes or tropical hide-a-ways in order to heal in peace, taking the family nanny along. In their absence, the gardener, maintenance man, chauffer-mechanic and housekeeper took care of the main residence.

Does this fit your definition of a "tragedy"? Let's check out Gram's '49, so we know we're on the same page. A tragedy is, "A literary composition, esp. a dramatic composition, which excites pity and terror by a succession of unhappy events, and in which, typically, the leading character is by some passion or limitation brought to a catastrophe."

Okay, what kinds of catastrophes excite pity or terror that cannot be resolved due to human passion or limitation?

Let's take a look at some tragic events – they are fictitious – and the different ways the upper crust and middle class resolve them.

Dramatic scenes are separated according to those that excite pity or terror:

Pity tragedy #1: Imagine if the middle-aged wife was abandoned when the husband ran away with the hot young thing.

Them:

"Dahling, my distress over that cur's indiscretion has driven me to close the Cape home early this summer and sail to Europe for shopping. It's so comforting."

Us:

"Sorry, kids, we need to re-roof the house more than you need new school clothes. You each get one new outfit – that's it."

Terror tragedy #1: A mouse is building its nest by gnawing on the family heirlooms. Sawdust is piling up on the floor, and the bold little critter is heard exploring the house at night. Telltale little black droppings confirm the trespasser's identity.

Them:

"Oh, that dreadful creature! Smithers! Do set up a barrier to prevent it from invading my bedroom. At sunrise, we will be moving to the Seaside Hotel until such time as the house is perfectly purged. Hasten."

Us:

"Oh, hell! Should I get a mousetrap or some poison?

Shit, the trap splatters guts all over. But, sometimes, once you poison 'em, they die between the walls and stink up the place..."

Pity tragedy #2: Due to her tireless contributions to the community, she is invited to be in the big Fourth of July parade. Oh, no! Her outfit is accidentally torn.

Them:

"Mayor Hansen! Do move over, please. The lace has been pulled loose from my Revolutionary War ball gown. I must have room on this float to settle it appropriately around me. In a moment, I shall need smelling salts. Let's see if I remember my princess wave from the high school homecoming parade."

Us:

"Okay, Janey, hold the school flag higher. It's dragging and getting dirty. Ricky, honey, stop hanging on my patriot costume, you're tearing it. Just hold my hand. Keep marching. If you can't make it the last few blocks, I'll carry you. Everybody smile and wave."

Terror tragedy #2: It's the middle of a harsh winter. A sleet storm has just coated everything with layers of ice.

Them:

"What do you mean, George, that it'll do no good to warm up the limo because we're snowed in? I refuse to be stranded! Simply warm up the rooftop landing pad instead. Then call Pilot Rogers to bring the helicopter over. I mustn't be late for my weekly luncheon at the Club."

Us:

"I'm sorry I'm late for work. The car wouldn't start. The neighbor came over and jumped it for me. I froze out there trying to scrape the ice off the windshield." (Shit ... I hope I don't have to take a half a vacation day for this).

Pity Tragedy #3: The economy has taken a dive. Business is bad. The family support your ex-husband has been faithfully sending dwindles as his income falls off.

Them:

"Can you believe that deserter is taking me to court to reduce the $20,000 a month alimony he owes me? And, threatening to sell the home on the Riviera in order to pay some corporate debts from the businesses he inherited? How will I maintain my current lifestyle?"

Us:

"Sis, I need your advice. My ex can't keep paying child support. It's either give up the house or get an additional part-time job. But, who will watch the kids? Man, is this little family screwed. What do you think about me asking mom and dad if the kids could stay with them? Just for the summer, of course."

<u>Terror Tragedy #3</u>: You've had a rotten toothache – in your eyetooth, right up front. You hate the dentist, but it'll only get worse.

Them:

"Thank God we have the best dentist money can buy. The state-of-the-art tooth extraction process he developed was completely painless. The replacement implant fits perfectly, and the color is an exact match for my other teeth. No one will ever know it's there!"

Us:

"I know I should have gone in sooner, but the benefits I get with my new job just kicked in. It was only a 90-day wait, but that was too long. Now the tooth is discolored. It'll have to be pulled and a false one made. But even my dental insurance won't fully cover expenses. Dammit, I look stupid!"

You may think that some of these situations are exaggerated. Of course, they are. We average people don't cuss as much as these tragedies show. Not all rich women are drama queens.

When it comes down to it, though, a wealthy woman

can hire or demand the work done. She doesn't have to know how to light a stove, cut the grass or change the oil in the car. Money gives her privilege: she won't wear herself out just to keep the basics going. Gram's '49 says it's part of Darwin's "natural selection," which is: "The natural process tending to cause the 'survival of the fittest' (that is, the survival of those forms of animals and plants best adjusted to the conditions under which they live), and extinction of poorly adapted forms."

In most middle-class families today, we work our butts off to adjust. Both adults need paying jobs to support their three-bedroom rambler in the suburbs, decent cars, annual vacation and special activities for the children. Being a divorced form of animal is a royal pain in the assets.

Add to that 100% of the responsibility for car maintenance, household chores and tree trimming. All while you're telling the kids to cheer up. Whew! Hard work actually had a lot of joy when shared with someone with whom you were building a future. Alone, it becomes the cause of massive resentment. The single head of household is now financially, physically and emotionally exhausted. What was once normal orneriness is cause for a major snap'itude.

"Adapting" takes on a whole new meaning.

So, how can the middle-class, middle-age woman move on? How can she take a college class to improve herself? Or, afford a weekend at a nudist colony scouting for a new love? Sometimes, *she can't.* She has to focus on building a new foundation for survival.

Therein lies the distinction.

Despite the stress and humiliation, and whatever the particulars, the abandoned rich are not threatened with losing their most basic needs for food and shelter. No sane person wants to take that away from them. But the impact of their loss, as bad as it is, still leaves them a step up on the survival ladder.

The scariest issue pertinent to modern adaptation is the cost of health care. The problem is most insurance comes attached to a job. If the primary breadwinner's company-sponsored insurance benefits stop, you are out.

Of course, serious diseases – such as the babbling one – can attack indiscriminately. Even those who can afford the healthiest lifestyles and personal trainers are not spared. When true tragedy hits, more money does translate into better medical care, though prescription meds can be a blow to anyone's budget.

The Affordable Care Act does take us toward being a truly "developed" nation. Even better, imagine if we could all be guaranteed health care through a tax fund. We could cut out the middleman insurance company. It would cost less overall *and* definitely shift the power balance away from the employer. Now the *boss* would need to tread lightly, because *we* wouldn't have to be trapped in a job we loathe.

Don't like your job? SCREW it – your health's not at stake. I think I'll be my own boss and work out of my home office as a freelance journalist. That guy thinks he'll follow the carnival and set up rides as the "tilt man." Maybe you'll work for a fledgling small business, because the boss has charisma. We'll all do whatever we damn well please. Quintessential freedom!

Employees will still strive to do a good job and pay taxes, but no longer be stuck choosing between security and freedom.

As my dear friend Benny advised me, anyone who gives up a little freedom for a little security deserves neither security nor freedom. Amen.

I suppose I really shouldn't complain. We "average" Americans still have it better than most of the world. To comfort myself for my lack of millions, I smile when I realize it relieves me of the responsibility of pretending I like fish eggs – or roe – also called "caviar" by society's "hoity-toity." The hoity-toity, according to Gram's old-fashioned '49, are: "Giddy; flighty; also, haughty; patronizing."

The first definition of "roe" is: "The eggs of fishes, esp. when still enclosed in the ovarian membranes." Just think of all those little whales that'll never get a chance to develop because fate has them wrapped in irresistible membrane munchies. Ptew! I'll be back in a minute, I think I'm gonna puke.

When I see my limburger-loving Gram in heaven, I'm going to ask her if she liked to eat roe. I hope she says, "No!"

Besides, it is a point of pride among middle-class people to refrain from being whiney, while admitting our society has largely brought a lot of these woes upon itself.

Part of this confusion might be based in the turmoil following the women's liberation movement. Though not a bra-burning fanatic, I was a raving lunatic over the inequities. We were all justified in our behavior and earned the right to be called "Ms." Who could resist the call to be a feminist?

#2 in Gram's '49 states that feminism is, "The theory, cult, or practice of those who advocate such legal and social changes as will establish political, economic, and social equality of the sexes." We witches wear "cult" as a badge of pride as we march for equality.

During my early 30s – in the late '70s – I was into the more combative form of women's lib. Like the time my boyfriend surprised me with a new used car after the old one finally crapped out. Instead of giving him a hug of grat'itude, I upbraided him for not asking me to pick out the car *I* wanted.

Just Average?

Here we are, three decades later, and things have improved tremendously. Women do have better – though not equal – pay and opportunities as men. We are still rarely hired as the #1 national prime-time TV news analyst, much less revered as a female Walter Cronkite; hence, "the most trusted woman in America." There *is* cause for celebration now that our country has seriously considered a viable female presidential candidate, but most media referred to her informally by her first name – while the males were more respectfully referenced by their last names or titles.

There is more work to be done, and what we've fought for can slide away.

We need to encourage the female rookie managers to stay in the game. They don't realize there was a time they would have been asked on a job application if they had a babysitter. Young working women can't take today's rights for granted. They need to recycle the power. Hire the best person – whether a hyster or testickle – at the best pay. Campaign. Have a LOUD voice. Vote. After all, if you don't vote, you can't bitch.

Things will never be perfect, but let's look at the progress we've made and give each other credit. It's sure better today because we have options, rather than being stuck in an unwanted role because of society's expectations. Our young women have better opportunities and they need to take advantage of them.

What's the trade-off?

It started when we lady boomers were young moms. We often had no choice but to get a paying job and drop the kids off at daycare. Maybe some of us would have preferred to be full-time homemakers. Conversely, most of *our* mothers had no choice but to be stay-at-home moms. Maybe some of them would have liked an out-of-home career. Both lifestyles are honorable.

It was easier for our parents, though, in the sense that each knew what her or his responsibilities were. The division of labor was clear. It is difficult when domestic job descriptions and financial roles are blurred.

In truth, I don't want to learn how to build a deck. I don't care if my old man can cook chili as well as I can. Ideally, *both* spouses are supposed to be capable of doing *everything*. How were we sucked into accepting – no, demanding – this lifestyle as desirable?

Imagine applying this superhuman model at a company where each employee was supposed to be the best salesperson, accountant, graphic designer, computer expert, forklift driver, administrative assistant, janitor and manager.

The boss says to all five members of her team: "This week, each of you is expected to bring on two new accounts. Then, everyone design a new product pamphlet, making sure to place media ads for our upcoming promotion. Next, develop new computer bookkeeping programs to make it faster for you to balance the ledger. Between greeting clients and answering the phones, be sure to check the lobby for cleanliness. I'm looking forward to hearing a week from today who loaded and delivered the most product."

It would be total frustration. No one would really be able to develop exceptional skills, and no one would be responsible or accountable.

I'm thinking that in our present state of home cohabitation, whether married or "living in sin," pressure is on both partners to be jack-of-all-trades. This is a fatal error. Lack of definition ultimately leads to competition. Why set ourselves up for failure?

Guys are no doubt as confused about these new roles as we are. They cheerfully offer to stay home with the kids so we can go out for a relaxing night with our friends.

Then, we overhear them explaining to the neighbor that they're "babysitting" tonight. Well, obviously, since we women don't "babysit" our *own* kids – we can't resist chastising the well-meaning guy for his thoughtlessness.

Gee, it's fun being a female chauvinist pig. Some of our biases are historically proven, such as "Women and children first" into the lifeboats. Most ladies apparently graciously accepted. Survivor recollections do not recount a lot of argument among the men as to who should be treated equally, with lots drawn to fairly determine who would stay on board the Titanic to rearrange the deck chairs and who would get into the life boats.

Would *that* qualify as HISassment – the male counterpoint to HERassment?

A sad modern example is the abuse against men that's promoted as humor under the guise of TV sitcoms. Here's a common scenario. The college friends are all out in the park playing a game of football. Isn't it funny when the gal kicks the guy in frustration, or throws the football smack at him, giving him a black eye? Ha. Ha. He's a manly man and takes it in stride. Ha. Ha. The ratings are climbing.

But imagine the reverse – the guy's kicking and hitting the gal, all in a good day's fun. Do I hear a hue and cry against the asshole?

Women always expect the guys to leave the toilet seat down. While this is a less important sexist fact, we need to get off our thrones. Imagine your significant male coming out of the bathroom all hot and bothered, and pouting, "You left the toilet seat down. Could you please be a little more considerate and leave it up?" Accompanied by an angry flush.

What a load of crap'itude!

It's actually not so much about the thoughtlessness of who leaves the seat up or down – it's about the physical torture of anyone having to touch the dirty disgusting thing to move it.

Invention Suggestion: how about a toilet seat lever operated with your foot.

Or a spring-loaded "Leave-a-Leak Behind" switch you push up or down on the tank?

Sometimes, ladies, we overwhelm *ourselves* because of our resistance to delegating.

Why, for example, do we cling to our house cleaning responsibilities when we could afford to hire a cleaner? What is liberated about *that*? Meanwhile, a guy drops the car off at the garage for a tune up so he's free to golf with his buddies.

Perhaps it's most sensible to agree on who's responsible for what. No one would be shoved into a corner, but the particular chores would not be as important as contributing a fair share of invaluable *time*.

Of course, being a feminist is not about being constantly confrontational. Most of us don't want to prove we can function *entirely* on our own. It does make more sense to thrive within a mutually supportive system.

I like men. Marriage can be wonderful. Many lady boomers are happily married. Others chose to stay satisfyingly single. What stimulates one woman can frustrate another.

Hopefully, you never regret the experiences which got you to where you are today. By choice or default, though, each of us has tasted the smoky singles scene.

Ever felt like a social piece of meat? Not the meat-stuck-in-your-teeth-meat that can mess up a date. I mean meat market meat, down and dirty.

"Meat market" is not in Gram's '49. ("Meatman" is, however, and may be related). Nevertheless, I'd like to propose that the meaning underlying today's slang expression originated long ago.

Although we may wish to forget it, there was a time

when young ladies each came with a dowry: "The money, goods or estate which a woman brings to her husband in marriage."

This was true among many civilizations – both raw and cultivated. Family stature, physical stamina and beauty were likely overriding assets. Personally, I think the women who came with goods, before money was invented, were especially interesting. Imagine the variety of treasures that must have meant. Could it be crops, cattle, skins, stone axes or jewels?

What is your wildest ancestral dowry dream?

Somehow, I fantasize that in a previous life, I was valued at two pigs and a cow. It's just a gut feeling. And, "two pigs and a cow" has a poetic ring, doesn't it?

By these standards, what is the average maiden worth in today's market? What would the non-sexist guy bring as his dowry?

If we already have food and shelter, would loyalty, brains, and a sense of humor be fixtures on the scale of modern meat? How do we go about attracting the most valuable partners in the first place?

It begs a related question – how do those wayward older guys get those hot young chicks? I hate to say it, but *it's because they can.* Sure, a hard-bodied fresh young pecker is more satisfying in the rack, but these older guys have superior dowries – even though they are convinced the hot young things like them for who they are.

Like preening peacocks they use their colorful feathers to capture a fresh fuzzy bush with whom to procreate. Thinking entirely with the lizard brain in their testickles, these vainglorious guys damn near worship "bush" in the sense that it is, "Uncleared or uncultivated country." They are indeed bushmen. A "bushman," is "A woodsman; ... one who lives in the 'bush'." Their motto is, "A bush in the hand is worth two birds."

What these bushmen don't know is *they* are the ones who are being captured – by smart lasses who see those colorful feathers as established careers, money to spend on fancy dinners and trinkets, and investments that translate into college tuition for the second set of kids.

The crown jewel on an old cock? He can provide the new wife with her own, custom-designed "execushack." An execushack is typically a four-story fake rock house situated on a relatively tiny but expensive waterfront lot. It's built just close enough to the water to block the views of the neighbors on either side. It's the nouveau riche woman's way of sticking her snoot in the air and saying, "Up yours."

The old money neighbors, who have seen other upstarts come and go, justifiably respond by blackballing the little wannabe from high society: "Smell *this*, sweetheart." They want to help the brat learn money may buy her survival – but it won't buy her *happiness*.

Chapter 9

HOPE SPRINGS ETERNAL

THE BOTTOM LINE

"HELLO, hello, hello, IS THERE ANYBODY IN THERE? JUST NOD IF YOU CAN HEAR ME. IS THERE ANYONE AT HOME?"

Pink Floyd's words ricochet around my minds these days. My vagina is not feeling "Comfortably Numb." She is still trapped in scar tissue, and I wonder – is revirginity a desirable trait in a lady boomer? Not able to find any conclusive research findings about this uncommon state, I am nevertheless determined to get properly waylaid – even if only once more.

Reflecting on the patient gentleman I last tried to be with, it suddenly occurred to me maybe it was not totally *my* lack of accessibility that made us incompatible. After all, he was the only one I'd tried to make it with. Maybe *he* was short on problem-solving talent.

Following this track logically meant that all I had to do was try it with another guy – or two – or three – until I found that mattress champion who could magically cultivate my bush. That durable man who would relish the challenge of bouncing around with obstructed – though previously cleared – now once again obstructed – but longing to be cleared – shrubbery.

It certainly shouldn't be hard to find some male lab rats to participate in my re-LAY-tion-ship experiment. To corroborate this assumption, think about the last time you were out with your girlfriends, enjoying a cocktail at your favorite spot.

There you are, in a conversation with the entertaining male a couple of barstools down. Soon, it's late and your friends are ready to go. As you stand up, you say sincerely to the guy, "Good night. I have certainly enjoyed your company. You're a very interesting person."

Rather than just say, "Thank you," he'll likely respond with, "You must come up to my place sometime." As he smiles at you sincerely, he offers you a hand and tightly squeezes yours.

Much to my surprise, Gram's '49 gives an adjectival form of "must" aka "musth": "Being in a condition of dangerous frenzy, usually connected with sexual excitement; – said of adult male elephants."

"Why, the very idea!" as Grandma used to say.

But, what if you were in the mood for a night of rampaging musth? Don't equal rights give an honest liberated woman the right to say, "Yes," without social fallout?

Most of us today would say males and females are treated similarly, no matter what. But, we're still learning. Here's a simple quiz to check your inclinations:

Q: An attractive single person who dates lots of different people and enjoys wild sex as a fun sport is a:

1. Stud
2. Slut
3. Both of the above.

The correct answer is #3, but I bet in your heart you don't think of stud and slut as describing the same behavior. Is there a female equivalent of a stud? Can a woman be deliciously slutty? What is the male version of a slut?

Let's check with our language authority: A "slut" is, "1. A slovenly woman, a slattern; 2. A lewd woman, a harlot; 3. A bitch." Whoa! Could have knocked me over with a feather! Looks like being a slut is strictly a womanly endeavor.

Checking out our modern day male equivalent, stud, we find it pertains to a post. Using our imaginations, however, we can apply other selected descriptions from Gram's '49, such as: "A kind of nail with a large head; an ornamental knob..."

"Stud" is also not to be mistaken for "stub," which is, "The short blunt part of anything after the larger part has been...used up; stocky, thickset, squat."

There is also "stud poker." Without going into detail, we know it fits better, so long as you pronounce it correctly. That's, "stud poke her."

Aha! This is the one! Stud is also, "A collection of horses, kept primarily for breeding; any male kept for breeding..."

"Stud" comes nowhere close to meaning male bitch. It is kind of sexist, though, when you apply stud terminology, "...kept...for breeding." There is no doubt, then, where the term "studbook" comes in: "A registry of the pedigrees and performance of horses."

I see an element of delicious fun, ladies. Should every one of us keep studbooks? We could compare our collections. Throw out the useless ornamental knobs. Highlight the large, functioning heads. If we're not sexually and emotionally satisfied, what will it matter? We'll keep studs purely for entertainment. At least we'll get nailed regularly. We can still continue with the scientific inquiries and make recommendations to our sister friends, just like men do with their slut encounters. Was he a stud or a stub? Hmmm...interesting.

Sadly, as we've proven, women who screw around are not studs. You can spontaneously sleep with him tonight or have another date with him tomorrow. Say "Yes!" now and you're relegated to an entry in his slutbook collection, to be shared by all his cronies. It may not be "fair" – it just

Just Average?

IS.

Damn! This means my bush cultivation project could result in a social identity of un-sportswoman-like conduct. I'm forced to scrub my search for a mattress champion(s).

Whether female or male, since the Garden of Eden, we can't resist sniffing each other out. Even the casual encounter at the bar illustrates a tentative inhaling, a relaxing atmosphere where we can investigate our compatible pheromones. Sniff, sniff. Sniff, sniff.

The truth is, we smell like anything but natural humans. For the last couple of generations, we've been brainwashed into believing that attraction to the opposite sex requires spending a fortune on products created to make us smell good. We slather, douche, rub and spray ourselves beyond recognition.

After all, what is a crotch if it isn't a Delicate Whisper? Who can be a member of the in-crowd if she doesn't sport Sea Breezes armpits? Can a woman be a *real* woman without a matching set of Morning Meadow shampoo, conditioner and soap? Cucumber & Lavender body lotion and powder are also necessities. Obviously, a thorough brushing with Star Bright toothpaste has to be followed with a gargle of Peppermint Pretty mouthwash. Of course, if we are going to win this race for survival of the fittest, we must dab on the same Lucky Seven Scent perfume worn by our favorite movie star. Slide on some flaming Strawberry Pout lipstick and voila!

We certainly smell...interesting.

Little do we know, but these products take on a life of their own. In the middle of the night, Mr. Cucumber Powder is dancing with Ms. Lavender Lotion on the vanity, while Master Soap is telling lewd jokes to Miss Deodorant. Madame Perfume meanwhile is standing to the side, acting all hoity-toity. But underneath it all, she's enjoying talking to herself about her younger days. Days spent in the caressing sunshine, growing more beautiful by the moment, attracting her own kind of stud – a King Bee.

All along, you thought you couldn't remember where you put all your smelly stuff. Somehow, *they* just moved...

Out with sweet perfume and sappy deodorant! To hell with weak, agreeable odors! In with scents that turn on our olfactory organs!

Today's females would absolutely benefit from wearing smells that make men paw and feel territorial. Experience tells us a new pigskin, perhaps gasoline, hot pizza, spicy chili and steak-on-the-grill would form a solid introductory line. To be sure, a scientific smell survey would be done among men first. They would have to be blindfolded so as not to be visually influenced by the women wearing the scents. After the initial product release, and based on popularity, new smells could be developed, such as beer-and-onion rings.

Developing scents for men to wear, on the other hand, is a bit more complicated. Real men, as we know, wear musky aftershave. Though "musk" may indeed awaken a primal attraction, it's a little hard core.

Do these guys know what they're wearing? Musk is extracted from the civet cat, which is, "A long-bodied, short-legged, catlike carnivorous animal (genera *Viverra Civettictis*), native to Africa."

Specifically, Gram's '49 refers to "civet" as, "A thick yellowish substance of strong musky odor, found in a pouch near the sexual organs of civet cats, and used as a perfume."

Eeewwwww!

Let's pause to gasp for a vote. Which is more palatable? The insect lac resin women spray on their hair or the civet musk men wear? Oh, my. To what extremes won't we go to be sexy? And, why isn't this information duly noted on our hairspray and aftershave bottles? Have you ever heard even the slightest hint about these secret ingredients in a TV commercial? Why hasn't this been investigated? Where is Sergeant Joe Friday when you need him?

Can we agree that musk is out? So, what's a guy to do?

Most women like roses, but what a wimpy way for a guy to smell! How about the scent of fresh-cut grass? The interior of a new car, dark chocolate, wine and light beer would be great starters. As indicated by sales, variations on these scents, such as adding nuts to the dark chocolate, could create high demand.

Are we witnessing the birth of a failsafe marketing venture? What if we launch our products under the new 21st century "Meat Market" label?

At least that says what it means. It's up front and honest!

Or, do we need to get back to the basics like our Homo erectus ancestors. You don't see cave people in docudramas worrying about hiding their sweaty hides or smelling sweet. Their idea of a good day was having enough food, shelter and sex to ensure continuation of the species.

Men focused on hunting, mating and fighting intruders. Women's work included foraging, tending the fire, and rearing the children. Life didn't even allow for the mental image of a two-week paid vacation, much less arguing about where to go.

Though the specific gender roles have evolved over the eons, men and women still *process information* differently from one another.

Some sociologists, however, cling relentlessly to the "blank slate" theory – the concept that men and women are born exactly alike in their heads, and behavioral differences are *all* learned. What a concept – we are all little blackboards to be written upon or, more appropriately, cell phones waiting to receive text messages.

Just take a look around you, and you will see this theory is bunk, a pure and simple fallacy. If all behaviors are learned, why do children raised in the same families have different personalities? My neighbors had a set of twins. One smiled a lot as a baby, but the other one screamed most of the time. Both have grown into beautiful young adults, but one still views life as half full while the other just knows it's half empty.

This is not to say we have no control over our behavior choices. Or that everything about us is nature. But, neither is it entirely social influence.

It's funny how humans are so pleased when we unravel the mysteries of other animals but refuse to acknowledge our own instincts. Nature made women and men different for our survival.

Why would we want men and women to be exactly alike, anyway? There's a vast difference between us. And, a "vas deferens," is "The excretory duct of a testicle; a spermatic duct, which is, in a man, a small but thick-walled tube about two feet long, greatly convoluted in its proximal portion."

Hold on a second. This is amazing. Gram's '49, our wise and silent partner, has demanded permission to speak! "Which of you ladies out there think that men's thick-walled tubes are interchangeable with your tubes? No? Then, stand back, and quit trying to tell nature its business. Harrumph."

Whoa! Gram's '49 got a little impatient there! But, just as men and women are physically different, there's also a vast difference in the way we think. Modern brain research points to inherent gender differences hardwired by nature.

We know the brain's hypothalamus, the area associated with sexual behavior, is larger in men. Yes, this substantiates the male elephant sexual frenzy application. Or, possibly it's the lizard brain, which is even more primitive. As much as we hate to admit it, overall, guys are better at reading maps. Ancient man had to excel at three-dimensional thinking when stalking mastodons and saber-toothed tigers.

Women are special, too. The bundle of nerves connecting our brains' right and left hemispheres – the corpus callosum – is often wider, allowing for greater cross-talk. This may be why we multitask so well, just like our CroMagWoman sisters before us. We can network at a business party, supervise the kids over the phone and give our husband a promising wink all at the same time.

Guys think more with one side of the brain at a time.

This is proof positive why women make better gynecologists.

If a man can't even talk while changing the oil in his car, imagine he's a doctor checking your womanly lubrication during a Pap smear.

You're lying up there on the white table, feet in the side harnesses, legs spread as daintily as possible under the privacy sheet. He begins the exam. As your brain hemispheres chatter back and forth to each other, you can't help but ask whatever comes to your mind. But, he honestly doesn't hear you.

"Doctor, I've been on medication for a year now. For lower abdominal pain."

"What?" he asks politely.

"The medication my last doctor prescribed for me. It only works for a little while. The pain keeps coming back."

"Uhm, it does?" He's busy zeroing in on the coordinates of your three-dimensional vaginal map, hunting for the target.

"Yes. And, it hurts so bad when my man and I have

sex, we don't even try, anymore. Please do something."

"Huh?" he frowns, losing focus while lifting his flushed pink face up from your bottom line. He tries hard, but we ladies are downright confusing – and he's no doubt confused.

But, once he comes up for air and can look you straight in the eye, you persistently start again.

In my case, I related the sad history of my unrelenting pelvic pain which led to the hysterectomy that only made matters worse.

His insightful response was, "Are you *sure* you want to have sex, anymore? This exam revealed no *physical* cause for the pain."

Unbelievable!!! I wanted to spit a "SCREW you" at him. Instead, I decided to give this guy one last chance.

"Yes," I countered. "I'd at least like the option. Revirgination is *not* a desirable trait at this time in my life."

In his infinite wisdom, the doctor impatiently explained the sexual barriers most women complained about were, in fact, *psychological*. They really didn't want to have sexual intercourse, anymore. He added, "Unfortunately, the majority of women like that ruin it for the few like you who actually *do* have physical pain."

I felt a snarl coming on.

I was stunned. That lowlife @!~#@~ doctor was trying to blame my afflicted sisters for his lack of diagnostic skill. It was the old divide and conquer. I began to look at him as an affable old-time rerun instead of a sage, sophisticated physician.

I asked him the obvious follow-up question, "And, precisely what battery of psychological tests are these women given, in conjunction with their physical exams?"

He frowned at me like I was a bad little girl.

"Then," I continued, "I suppose that's also true of men

with erectile dysfunction. The majority of it is psychological. They don't want to have sexual intercourse, anymore. Their complaints ruin it for the few men who actually have a physical problem."

"No, no," he condescendingly corrected me, employing a most demeaning pat'pat'pat'itude. "That's completely different. And, by the way, you can eliminate that scar tissue by simply pressing down on it with your finger from time to time."

"Just press on it," I mimicked.

Suddenly, I saw before me a man who had taken the HippoCritic Oath.

I couldn't help it. I indignantly asked, "Well, why don't you offer me some heavy-duty, magical mood altering medication? If by chance I'm cured by some voodoo queen, I can donate the leftover magic back to your clinic for other women in denial? It won't be wasted." The sarcasm dripped acid.

After he stomped out, I just had to ask myself if understanding women's bodies was a low priority in the gynecology field. How about a thoughtful cure instead of a quick cover up?

I wonder if our pelvic pain would get more attention if it were an election year. Vagina politics should matter as much as erectile dysfunction. With enough pressure on our electorate, could money and talent be legislated to fund research on female private parts problems?

Hello, could anyone find a better solution than my hysterectomy? It did not get rid of the nasty pain, but in fact resulted in scar tissue aka my hymen grew back and made my vagina impassable. Even after that useless surgery to have the scar tissue removed, when I visited the "I- thought-we-were-compatible" gentleman, we still could not achieve lift off because my stubborn hymen had grown back again. Dammit! I need my life back!

Oops! Sorry about the "...hysteria...wild outbreak of emotionalism." My minds got into an impromptu meeting, and everyone was bitching at once.

My intuition tells me this is not an unsolvable problem. We must push them to probe further: "If it *isn't* what it *was* diagnosed to be, it *is* what it *wasn't* diagnosed to be." In fact, that's the path my primary doctor – a General Practitioner – takes. He has an absolutely positive influence on my health. Whatever kind of issue I go in to see him for – like bloody knees from a fall on a rugged sidewalk – he takes the action steps to check them thoroughly to determine the extent of the injury, cleans them up, advises for future care, including a prescription if needed. A GP has a very challenging career. For any mysterious pains – wherever they are – he checks thoroughly and explains to me the possibilities of the causes and related treatments. He has to consider more than one absolute and, if the first path doesn't totally work, we may test a bit further and apply a different path and prescription. GPs can't get stuck on a single path aimed at surgery.

Surgery can result in very positive outcomes. But, it can also be too much of an exploration...an "educated guess." Maybe they are human, after all, and we shouldn't expect them to be God.

It's just that some specialists – male and female – seem to get into a stubborn rut with their jobs, just like the rest of us. Why, if they are taking continuing education classes to learn about break-through advances, do they cling to outdated remedies? After all, it'd take time to be trained in modern pain medicine, diagnoses and procedures. Let's daydream about joining the Kiss My Ass club, instead. We'll just stick to those old-fashioned fixes like hysterectomies and magical meds. After all, we've already got a lucrative business going – why change now?

Even when you do succumb to the useless hysterectomy, they may take the uterus but not the ovaries. They don't advise us lady boomers that our ovaries will soon "shrivel right on schedule." Later, you're told they'll need to be removed, anyway. You get an estimate for more "necessary" work...just like on your car repairs.

Da Hell! Rich and poor, crotch sisters unite!

We need gynecologists who think outside the box!

Just as I'm about to write off the "experts," I get a reality check from my daughter – yes, that young lady who'd dumped Hollywood – and a future Academy Award – to go back to Minnesota and study science and medicine. Amazingly, she didn't give me the "TMI" when I'd told her the possible root of the pain in my uterus and vagina. Her college degrees included neurology and epidemiology courses, and now her focus is on global patient access and improvement. Wow! When you let 'em fly, they soar!

She took it upon herself to do an online search for help for Mama, which revealed the existence of a pelvic pain pioneer doing some unusual research. And, he's a man! Will he come galloping to my rescue, wearing a white hat and mask?

My GP checks it out and gives me a referral.

This pelvic pain doctor takes my problem seriously. He determines that it is a nerve problem, possibly activated by that sports injury from the year of living deliciously sinfully. You know, back when my hot date lowered the bed, and WHAMMO! All that passionate bouncing and pushing and helicopulating pissed off those, "bands of tissue that connect parts of the nervous system with the other organs, and conduct impulses...*strained every nerve...*"

I'm suffering from "pudendal nerve entrapment," which I'd never heard of. I had to check Gram's '49 for more insight on this. "Pudendum" is a derivative of "pudere," which means, "...that of which one ought to be ashamed. The external organs of generation, sometimes only of the female; the vulva."

Well, naturally, it just would be limited to females, wouldn't it? At this point, I don't even want to know any more. How can we women be so sensitive about terms like "mankind" vs. "humankind," yet not even be aware that our private parts are deeply rooted in shameful, hysterical terminology?

For my own sanity, I had to confront the doctor.

Bless him. He explained that today's definition of "pudendal neuralgia" has neither gender bias nor insult attached. It can be the cause of chronic pelvic pain in both men and women and can include a bundle of other problems, including sexual dysfunction.

No shit and shit howdy! I was already into forced sexual dysfunctioning! What else can you tell me, Doc?

This paragon of modern medicine kindly informed me not only of a new, improved diagnosis, but also solution options! He had completed successful, helpful surgeries to release those trapped nerves on many patients. The doctor shows me testimonials from patients who flew in from around the world and found help. The only problem is that many are not in English. Whatever. I am desperate to believe him!

But, for me, he thoughtfully suggested we try a different path before going to the surgery. It's a series of deep injections through the butt cheeks, aimed at critical nerves. They'll hurt, yes, but it's absolutely worth it. And, I have to stay open to coming back for future shots – or surgery – as necessary.

I schedule the treatment.

I wouldn't exactly say the shots "hurt." I couldn't even say they "hurt real bad." I'd have to say the pain was somewhere between, "What in the hell did I do this for?" and, "Mom, where are you when I need you?" But, I tearfully suffer through it. I have to think of it as an investment in my future!

Afterwards, the first test is passed when the anesthetic wears off. There's no pain...*yet.* I wait for it to rear its ugly head.

Gone. It's *gone!*

I'm starting to feel both relieved and guilty.

I reconvene a meeting of my minds. I admit I was wrong to slam doctors by gender. I have got to pull my head out of my ass! A humble apology is in order.

"Mea culpa!"

But those other clueless doctors who perform useless hysterectomies and stitch us too tight need their own attitude adjustments. Out of frustration come action steps. They will soon be receiving terse notes from me, reprimanding them for staying in the cave as the rest of the world evolved. They'll get orders to attend a seminar on pelvic pain management. If my stitching article is published by then, well, they'll each be the lucky recipient of an autographed copy. It'll be signed with a double V – my new personal logo – "*VV*" – vagina victory!

My next stop is to get rid of that stubborn hymen-like scar tissue caused by that needless surgery. But this will take longer than anticipated. Instead, he directs me to a physical therapist who specializes in this area.

I admit I was reticent about regular appointments that could stretch out for months before I felt confident the PT would help. Right away, the PT emphasized how the nerves are related in many areas of the body, and she explained the approach she was going to take. She had me lie on a comfy treatment table with a sheet over my lower body. She began massaging the ligaments stretching inside my legs from just below my pelvis. Other days, she'd have me lie on my side while she worked on my butt. At each visit, she'd put medicinal cream on the fingers of her gloves and penetrate my vagina – or another area – very calmly explaining everything to me, and always asking if I were comfortable – making sure I knew to tell her if I felt she was pushing too hard. She also stretched my scar tissue.

After several appointments, I began to feel better. I had hope! Hope this would indeed be the cure for – or at least significantly abate – my pain. She also explained the necessity of my doing outside leg stretches – and inside vaginal stretches – at home. I got a prescription for some cream via my GP.

Then, I snuck to the nearest porno shop for some assistance. There, I saucily approached the clerk as if I were looking for a whopping dildo for a wild night with a kinky partner. What I'm really doing is shopping for a "just average" fake penis I can insert little by little, centimeter by centimeter, inch by inch, night after night, all alone, until my vagina is stretched into usable shape.

At first, I try to imagine I'm having fun with the dildo. In reality, I'm gritting my teeth and muttering: "Just shove it."

Eventually, though, Dil and I become more than friends. I discover that he's no simple-minded meat substitute. He's a master at his craft. I develop a lot of respect for Mr. Do and write him into my studbook. Like those peonies, my dormant vagina begins to blossom again. I spread some of the cream to my pulsating clitoris. Oh, my, I do still have sexual sensations.

The true test is if I can exorcise my old sports injury ghost through some joyful bedroom gymnastics including hugs and slurpy kisses from someone other than myself.

Who you gonna call? You got it – my patient gentleman – the one who's been stumped twice. The last man I tried to be with. The man who could not be blamed for faulty probing because he had attempted the job valiantly.

Hope springs eternal. My knight is willing to take a stab at it.

I dye my hair a warm red – all of it. I rat it just a little – a sophisticated tease somewhere between Helmet Hair and Hippo Hair. I spray on a bit of lac resin to keep it in place. The anticipation builds as I strap on my custom-made Real Woman nippleless bra – I adjust – my pale pink eyes are looking ahead, not down. I put on a tight blue sweater that shows off my perky rosebuds and bitchy red hair. I pull on my low-cut boots and roll up my jeans to emphasize my firm calves. A dab of Lucky Seven Scent perfume is next. Then, a last minute check to be sure there's no meat stuck between my teeth. It's a go. I slide on some Strawberry Pout lipstick and grab my Viking helmet.

Last, but never least, I put on my ATTITUDE.

I am feeling deliciously sinful for the first time in a long time. I jump on Baby and hit the road. I'm in the wind. I feel those irreverent vibrations. Fun is a personal responsibility, and by the time I knock on his door, I am tingling.

My man answers with his muscular chest bared. Taking my hand, he leads me to the bedroom. His smoldering look says, "Lay down." My clothes fall off by themselves. We sprawl out together. The sheets are cool. He's hot.

Ever so tenderly, he licks my lips. I shiver as he caresses my hardening pink eyes. I close my other eyes. Anticipation, dread, longing and more all surged through me at once.

The initial tingling develops into a full out thrilling sensation

Now he's on top, diligently probing with his long,

luscious rod. I am optimistic. I keep kissing his neck and rubbing his parts, trying to keep him excited during the excavation effort. I am beginning to fear this is "Cherry Picker," season three.

Then, I peek through my eyelashes. It's not the patient gentleman hovering over me! It's *Benny*, the love of my other life.

Swept by long-lost emotions, I feel my belly firing up like a Franklin stove. The sparks fly as I thrust my hips into his lightning rod. He pins me to the sheet, and with one final push, my hymen is liberated.

Squeezing me tightly, the passionate patriot whispers in my ear. "My dear girl, remember, as with chess, the importance of not being discouraged in our state of affairs. Timing is life. To become independent of me – the past – you need to become less independent of the possibility of love in *this* life. You have atop you a patient gentleman who's right before the wind with all his studding sails out.

"My lovely," he whispered, "I'll miss you terribly, but it's time that you embrace *him*. *Now*."

"Now! *Now!*" I cry out. My basest instincts take over, and my hips uncontrollably shift into tornado gear. I can't stop embracing my patient man as the primal scream tears itself from my throat.

"Yes, yes, YES! *I'm free! I'm free!*"

When I open my eyes, it's the puzzled gentleman asking, "Was it good for you?"

"It's never been like *this* before," I assure him.

Trust me. It was anything but just average.

"RIDE SAFE!"

Acknowledgements

Yes, I admit I wrote this book, and that parts are real and parts are fiction. Yet I can't say enough about thegenuine support and inspiration I've gotten through life from family and friends, including:

The love and guidance of *my wonderful, fun and loving, parents* – *My Mom*, who always roared for us kids when we needed it. And, And *my Dad*, who sternly taught us to meet and beat challenges;

The wisdom of *my brother, Gary,* who so sagely said, "Timing is life!" and the encouragement of *my brother, Steve,* who regularly reminded me to pause and, "Savor the moment!"

Colleen aka "CSea" for her insightful questions about my odyssey as we reflected together;

Buddy, a rugged yet sharing guy who's creative in so many ways. When we get together, his presence still reminds me of the Key West '60s and the island life we shared;

My kids, Jason and Meredith, each taking their own professional and personal paths to success and supporting me in mine. And, of course, *my talented grandkids*, who make me smile and laugh more than anyone.

The ongoing sharing between me and my friend, awesome author, *Julia Robinson Shimizu,* across the miles from SoCal to MN and back;

Last, but not least – my heartfelt appreciation to *Mr. Shirrel Rhoades* for encouraging me to be me in my writings.

Thank you for reading.

Please review this book. Reviews help others find Absolutely Amazing eBooks and inspire us to keep providing these marvelous tales.

If you would like to be put on our email list to receive updates on new releases, contests, and promotions, please go to AbsolutelyAmazingEbooks.com and sign up.

About The Author

Allison Seaborn is twice-divorced, a mother-in-law, and a grandma. Just like many of her lady boomer sisters, she has started over emotionally and financially – learning from both success and failure. With an M.A. in Speech Communication from the University of Minnesota, she has taught community college courses in Interpersonal Communication. Writing and public speaking have also been at the core of her "other" career as a Director of Development/PR/Fundraising/Special Events/Volunteers for various nonprofits.

The New
Atlantian Library

New AtlantianLibrary.com
or AbsolutelyAmazingEbooks.com
or AA-eBooks.com

Made in the USA
San Bernardino, CA
02 May 2017